RIVALS IN LOVE

Bryony becomes private secretary to Justin, a charismatic but moody novelist. She finds him attractive — until she meets Rowan, his charming cousin. The two men have been estranged for years since they and Eleanor, whom they both loved, were caught up in a tragedy. Bryony risks Justin's wrath in her attempts to bring about a reconciliation between the cousins. But then she faces a dilemma — which man does she really love? And will history repeat itself?

Books by Toni Anders
in the Linford Romance Library:

A LETTER TO MY LOVE
DANCE IN MY HEART

TONI ANDERS

---◆---

RIVALS IN LOVE

Complete and Unabridged

LINFORD
Leicester

First published in Great Britain in 2005

First Linford Edition
published 2008

British Library CIP Data

Anders, Toni
    Rivals in love.—Large print ed.—
Linford romance library
1. Love stories
2. Large type books
I. Title
823.9'2 [F]

ISBN 978–1–84782–070–9

Published by
F. A. Thorpe (Publishing)
Anstey, Leicestershire

Set by Words & Graphics Ltd.
Anstey, Leicestershire
Printed and bound in Great Britain by
T. J. International Ltd., Padstow, Cornwall

This book is printed on acid-free paper

First Impressions

Bryony brought the car to a stop at the foot of a short flight of stone steps and climbed out stiffly. The journey from Wales had been long and her little car wasn't very comfortable. She stretched and took a deep breath of fresh country air.

Above her rose the honey-coloured stonework and huge windows of Greston Tower. The heavy front door opened and a girl of seventeen or eighteen flew down the steps, a welcoming smile on her pretty face.

'Bryony — you must by Bryony. At last! I've been looking out for you for the past hour.' She had thick fair hair and bright blue eyes which danced with anticipation.

Bryony glanced at her watch in consternation. 'I'm not late, am I? Mr Sancerre said lunchtime.'

'Don't worry about Justin. He's gone out. I'm going to look after you. Oh, my name's Heidi, by the way.'

'Gone out? But . . . '

'Don't worry,' the girl said again. She linked her arm in Bryony's and drew her up the steps towards the door. 'You'll see him at dinner.'

An older woman in a grey dress and white apron appeared in the doorway.

'Sorry, Miss Heidi — I didn't hear a car.'

'Mrs Buckley, this is Bryony Redland, the new secretary. Mrs Buckley is our housekeeper and the best cook in Worcestershire.' Heidi performed the introductions with ease. 'Come with me, Bryony, and I'll show you your room. Oh, give me your car keys, will you?'

She handed the keys to the housekeeper. 'Ask Buckley to bring Miss Redland's cases in and move the car, please, Bucks.'

The older woman gave her a fond smile. 'Of course, Miss Heidi, and there'll be coffee in the morning-room in ten minutes.'

Bryony was swept up the staircase on a wave of chatter.

'I can't tell you how glad I am that you've come to be Justin's secretary. His old one — Miss Gladstone — was a dragon. Didn't approve of me at all. But we'll be friends, I know. I really need someone near my age. Everyone's so old.'

'But Mr Sancerre isn't old, is he?'

Heidi grimaced. 'He's nearly thirty-eight! That's not exactly young.'

They had turned down a thickly-carpeted corridor at the top of the stairs and stopped at a door.

'You open it,' Heidi urged. 'I want to get your reaction.'

Smiling, Bryony pushed open the door.

'Oh, it's lovely,' she exclaimed spontaneously.

'Thank goodness for that,' said Heidi. 'I thought you'd find it very dull. I told Justin he ought to brighten it up a bit but he never takes any notice of me.'

Bryony took in the silver-grey striped wallpaper and dove-grey carpet. Deep plum-coloured curtains swayed in the breeze at the open window, wafting the scent of roses into the room. On the bed lay a thick coverlet of the same shade.

'It's a lovely colour combination,' said Bryony, 'and the flowers are wonderful.' Bowls of pale pink blooms echoed the pink of the lampshades.

'Your bathroom's through here.' Heidi threw open a corner door to reveal the same colour scheme.

Bryony crossed to the window. The room was at the back of the house and she looked out over the shrubs and flowers of an extensive garden. Happily, she breathed in the scent of a thousand blossoms.

Heidi joined her. 'Justin loves gardening,' she said. 'Not that he's exactly hands on himself, but he plans it all.'

'Is Mr Sancerre your . . . ?'

'I'm his ward,' said Heidi. 'So's my

brother, Lance. Our parents died when we were small. Justin has been in charge of us ever since, him and an aunt in London. But she's elderly and we hardly see her now. Justin was my father's best friend and we're a bit short of relatives. It's not so bad for Lance; he's three years older and a boy, so Justin thinks he can look after himself. But he suffocates me!'

Bryony looked at the furious young face and wanted to smile, but didn't dare. Heidi was deadly serious.

Then, just as suddenly, the younger girl's mood changed.

'Come on. Mrs Buckley will have the coffee ready. D'you want to wash your hands or anything?'

'My cases?' Bryony looked towards the door.

'Buckley — he's the gardener — will bring them up. You can sort them out later.'

★   ★   ★

'So how did you come to hear of this job?' asked Heidi. 'Justin told me yesterday that his new secretary would be arriving today, that her name was Bryony, and that she was a cousin of Lance's best friend — but nothing else.'

Bryony stirred her coffee slowly and smiled. They had just finished a delicious lunch. She was full of chicken pie and baked apples and cream and felt comfortable and mellow

'I'd better start at the beginning,' she said. 'My father was an actor. Not a famous one but usually busy. I was his personal assistant — you know, I typed his letters, arranged bookings at theatres, booked hotels, that sort of thing, and generally looked after him. We travelled all over the country. We even went to America several times. It was a fascinating life . . . '

Heidi looked at her curiously. 'So what happened?'

'He died.' Bryony said simply, her voice quiet. 'One night, a year ago. On stage.'

'How awful for you!' Heidi put a hand on her arm. 'And your mother?'

'She left us when I was small.' Bryony's voice was flat. 'I haven't seen her since.'

The two girls sat in silence for a moment, then Bryony took a deep breath.

'I went to live with my Aunt Margaret and Uncle Chris and my cousin Simon in Wales. I'd done history at university so I took a job as a history teacher at a small private school.'

'I'd hate to be a teacher,' Heidi put in with feeling.

'I didn't enjoy it either,' Bryony confessed. 'It was so dull compared with my previous life. Then one day, your brother came to see Simon. We were all talking together and he mentioned that his guardian was looking for a secretary for six months . . . '

'The dragon's having an operation,' Heidi put in.

'When he said that his guardian was

Justin Sancerre, the novelist . . . '

'You were interested,' Heidi supplied.

'I certainly was! Lance telephoned Mr Sancerre straight away and I was offered the job. No interview, nothing. I couldn't believe it.'

'Justin has a high opinion of Lance. If Lance thought you'd do, Justin would be satisfied,' Heidi commented.

'Lance said that although Mr Sancerre was a novelist he was taking some time off from fiction to research his family history and write a book on that.' Bryony shrugged. 'I supposed my history knowledge helped to sway him.'

'I'm glad it did,' said Heidi, with satisfaction. 'Just think, he could have found another dragon!' She pushed back her chair. 'Would you think I was dreadful if I left you alone this afternoon? I have to see someone.'

'Of course not. I have to unpack my things anyway. And perhaps I'll take a walk round the garden. It looks so beautiful.'

★   ★   ★

When she went upstairs, Bryony found her bags and cases lined up in the centre of her room.

Unfastening the largest, she began to shake out garments and hang them in the spacious wardrobes. But a shaft of sunlight across the bedroom floor made her glance towards the windows. How could she stay indoors on such a lovely afternoon?

Five minutes later, she was sauntering down the drive. She didn't know what made her walk in that direction rather than into the garden. Perhaps the burning sun on the back of her neck made the cool corridor of trees overhanging the drive more inviting.

The drive ended in a wide grassy space at the end of the lane. To the left, a low wooden fence edged the shrubbery of the Tower.

To her disappointment, there was nothing to see but fields and trees. To the left, the lane stretched away into the distance; to the right, it curved round a bend. When she investigated, that, too, revealed nothing of interest. There wasn't a building in sight. She would be dependent on her car to find out what, if any, interesting places the area had to offer.

She returned to the little fence and perched uncomfortably on its uneven top. A bee buzzed gently near her ear. The birds were almost silent. It was so peaceful — until a car shot round the bend and jolted to a stop on her piece of grass.

She was so startled that she lost her balance and toppled off the fence, letting out a yell as she landed awkwardly on one knee.

The car door flew open, a man leapt out and she felt herself being lifted to her feet. The arms were muscular and firm, the musky aftershave on the cheek near hers intoxicating.

'I'm so sorry! I didn't expect to see anyone there. There's *never* anyone there.' The voice was light and cheerful.

'But shouldn't you be prepared, just in case?' she retorted. 'Flying round corners at that speed is dangerous.' She glared at him.

'Are you hurt?' He had captured her arm and was bending her elbow up and down, but she snatched it away.

'Leave me alone!'

'You fell on your knee. Let me check it.' His hand firmly grasped her knee and pressed, and again she snatched herself away.

'Get off! How dare you! Who do you think you are — some sort of doctor?'

'Some sort,' he agreed. 'A vet, actually. A bone is a bone, whether it's yours or a heifer's.'

Despite herself, she began to laugh.

'Very elegant. I've never been compared with a heifer before.'

'That's better.' He was facing her and holding both her elbows and she found she didn't mind. The face before her was suntanned, the hair dark blond streaked with sunlight; the eyes, under straight brows, were bright like his voice.

Slowly he released her and held out his hand. 'I'm Rowan,' he said.

'Rowan what?'

He grinned. 'Oh, Rowan's enough for now. And you are — ?'

'Bryony,' she said. 'Bryony Redland. There's no mystery about me.'

'All right — Rowan Darke. And are you staying at Greston Tower or were you just passing?'

'I'm living here for a while. I'm Justin Sancerre's new secretary,' she explained.

Bryony saw the strange look that crossed his face.

'Do you know him?' she asked eagerly. 'It sounds silly but he offered me the job even though we'd never met.'

'I know him.' Rowan turned towards the car, plainly intending to make no further comment.

'What's he like?' Bryony persisted, following him. 'What sort of person is he?'

She couldn't see his face as he opened the rear door of the car and reached inside for a cat basket.

'I think you'd better wait and find that out for yourself,' he returned evasively. 'I don't want to influence you. Have you met Nanny Flake?'

She knew he was changing the subject and was intrigued.

'Nanny Flake?' she echoed.

'A very dear old friend of mine. Come with me and I'll introduce you. You might find her a useful — ally.' He handed her the basket. 'Perhaps you'd like to carry this.'

She peeped inside. Two slanting, emerald eyes looked up at her in a fluffy, tortoiseshell face.

'Oh, what a sweetheart!' she exclaimed.

'He's got the same colouring as you,' Rowan commented. 'Green eyes and tortoiseshell hair.'

She blushed. 'Is he for Nanny Flake?'

'He is. Come on, we'll go through the shrubbery.'

Carrying the kitten with care, Bryony followed Rowan into the trees. She was puzzled. Parking at the bottom of the drive, approaching the house through the shrubbery — it was as if he didn't want to be seen. And why had he referred to Nanny Flake as an ally? Why should she need an ally?

But Rowan was striding ahead and she didn't want to shout the questions after him.

They emerged at the side of the house near the tower which gave it its name. Rowan produced a key and unlocked the door at the base of the tower. Stairs curved upwards. They climbed up and arrived at a tiny landing. Facing them was a pillar-box red front door.

Rowan knocked; three loud knocks and three soft ones.

'Secret signal,' he confided with a grin.

'Rowan?' A voice came from behind the door. 'I was just thinking about you.'

The door was opened by a tiny old lady in a vivid scarlet trouser suit. Bryony blinked. The outfit was quite unexpected on a lady of such advanced years: The face, wrinkled as a walnut, and the tiny claw-like hands suggested that she was well over eighty. But the eyes had the intelligent sparkle of a young woman. Bryony liked her immediately.

'I've brought you a visitor, Nanny,' said Rowan, drawing Bryony forward.

'Good. I love visitors!'

'I'm sure you'll be seeing a lot of her. This is Bryony Redland, Justin's new secretary.'

'Then why is she with you?' The expression on the old face was shrewd.

'Never mind about that. We met at the bottom of the drive and she helped me carry a new friend for you.'

The old lady seemed to notice the cat basket for the first time.

'Rowan! You remembered!'

'Of course I remembered. Now sit down in the armchair.'

Rowan opened the basket, extracted the kitten and placed it carefully on Nanny Flake's lap — where it instantly curled up and went to sleep.

'The little darling,' crooned the old lady. 'I lost my old cat a few weeks ago,' she told Bryony, 'and Rowan promised me a new kitten.'

'Training him will keep you out of mischief,' he chuckled. 'Now, I must go, and Bryony must get back in case Justin returns and wants to see her.'

'Come and see me any time,' the old lady said. 'We'll have a cup of tea and a gossip.'

'But how do I get in?' Bryony turned to Rowan, remembering the key he had used on the tower door.

'There's a connecting door to the house. Come on, I'll show you.'

Bryony said goodbye to Nanny Flake and followed Rowan through a short passage to another door. He opened it on to one of the corridors in the main house.

'This corridor faces the one that leads to the guest rooms — that's where yours is, I imagine,' he said. 'Don't forget, Nanny will be glad to see you any time. She doesn't go out and visitors are her link with the outside world. Goodbye, Bryony, I'm sure we'll meet again soon.'

The door closed abruptly. It was as though Rowan was afraid someone might see him.

★　★　★

She set off down the corridor, passed the top of the stairs and continued down the opposite corridor to her bedroom. The house was quiet. She wondered where Heidi was and whether Justin Sancerre had returned.

In her room, she finished unpacking her cases, wondering as she hung each garment in the wardrobe whether she had brought enough clothes. Greston Tower was grander than she had anticipated and Heidi had mentioned that she would be expected to dress for dinner. Perhaps the other girl would take her shopping in the nearest big town — wherever that was. The Tower was quite remote and she couldn't imagine shops nearby.

But what should she wear tonight? She had to make the right first impression on her new employer.

If only she knew what he was like. What would he expect her to wear? She had a smart trouser suit, but he might be the sort of man who disapproved of trousers for formal wear.

At last she settled on a calf-length black skirt and a ruffled Victorian blouse. Neat, old-fashioned and safe, she thought.

She enjoyed preparing for the evening in her own small bathroom, though there was a slight feeling of apprehension in the pit of her stomach. She lathered herself lavishly with the expensive shower gel, revelling in the luxurious experience. The scent lingered on her skin as she towelled herself dry.

She was buffing her nails when Heidi knocked on the door and looked in.

'Oh, good, you're ready. Justin hates us to be late.'

'He's back then?'

'He got back an hour ago with Carla. She's staying for dinner, unfortunately.' The girl made a face.

'Who's Carla?'

'Carla Willard. I'm afraid you'll see a lot of her. She thinks of herself as Justin's girlfriend, but she's only a friend. He sometimes needs a partner for dinners and so on and she fits the bill. She's glamorous and quite amusing, though very bitchy. But he'll never marry her, whatever she thinks. He's not the marrying kind.'

They descended the stairs together. At the bottom Bryony paused to study the portrait of a strikingly beautiful Indian girl.

She looked inquiringly at Heidi.

'Family mystery,' said the younger girl. 'I expect Justin will tell you. She's sure to be in the book.'

They carried on to the drawing-room, which was empty except for a youngish woman lounging elegantly on the couch. This must be Carla Willard,

Bryony guessed.

Heidi effected the introductions, but although Carla Willard smiled, she didn't extend her hand. Bryony returned the smile and sat in an armchair opposite.

As Carla turned away from her and gazed out of the window, Bryony was able to study her unobserved. The other girl's features were too sharp for beauty, but her eyes, her best feature, were large and bright. A mop of red curly hair reached to her shoulders. Her dress was a striking kingfisher blue, a colour Bryony loved but would never dare to wear.

The only sound in the room was the flick of pages as Heidi studied a fashion magazine.

Suddenly the door opened again, and on the threshold stood a tall man in beautifully cut clothes. His thick fair hair was sun-streaked. His eyes, under their straight eyebrows, had a quizzical expression. He was extremely hand-some. Bryony caught her breath. He was also, allowing for a slight difference in colouring, the double of her new friend, Rowan.

'Justin, darling, there you are,' drawled Carla. 'We were becoming really quite hungry.'

'I don't believe I'm late,' Justin returned mildly. 'It's just seven now.'

Bryony took a surreptitious glance at the mantel clock which began to chime seven.

Carla rose from her chair expectantly, but Justin sidestepped her and crossed the room to Bryony.

'My new secretary, I believe?' he said, and held out an arm. 'May I take you into dinner?'

Bryony didn't dare to look at Carla but she could feel spikes of irritation coming from the other girl. Carla Willard would never offer her friendship, she knew.

Ignoring Carla, Justin settled Bryony into the chair on his right and took his place at the head of the table. Carla took the chair on his left and Heidi sat at the bottom, facing him.

Bryony became aware of a tension in the group and wished there could have been more people there. She started to eat her melon, relieved that it was something she enjoyed.

As Mrs Buckley removed the first course plates, Justin turned to Bryony. It was the moment she had been dreading.

'Well, Miss Redland, as we haven't had a formal interview, you've had no opportunity to question me about your new position. What would you like to know?'

Bryony smiled shyly, but couldn't reply. This handsome, famous man had reduced her to nervous silence. How would she manage when she had to work in close proximity to him every day? Perhaps, after a while, familiarity would breed, not exactly contempt, but an ability to accept him as just another man, but at the moment she couldn't get past the fact that he was quite gorgeous!

He was speaking again and she forced herself to concentrate on his words, not his looks.

'I want you to help me with the research for a book I'm writing about one of my ancestors, Sir Andrew Darke,' he was explaining.

Darke. That was Rowan's name. They looked alike and they had the same family name — yet Rowan had acted very strangely when he had asked about Justin.

'I understand you have an interest in history and drama?' he asked, and Bryony nodded. 'That could be very useful.'

I can't just smile and nod, Bryony thought desperately, conscious of Carla watching her with a sardonic smile on her face. Say something, she urged herself.

'History is my special interest,' she managed. 'I'll enjoy helping with that.' It was easier now she had started. 'Was Sir Andrew famous?'

'Not famous, no, but he had an

interesting life. I think it's worth recording. And,' he smiled, 'I want a break from writing fiction.'

'That will disappoint your fans. I love your books. I've read them all,' she told him impulsively, and hoped she didn't sound too fawning.

He smiled his thanks.

'I have another duty for you which should be more fun, although I hope you won't see it as a duty. I'm hoping you'll be a companion to Heidi. There are so few young girls in our neighbourhood.'

'I'm sure we'll be great friends.' Bryony smiled at the younger girl. 'We got on very well together today.'

'Good.' He sat back in his chair and helped himself from a dish held out by Mrs Buckley. 'Of course, when Heidi goes to finishing school next summer, she'll make plenty of friends there.'

'I shan't be going to finishing school. I've told you.' Heidi's voice was quiet and determined. 'And you can't make me.'

Bryony looked at Heidi and was startled by the mutinous look on her face.

'Heidi wants to be a model,' Carla explained in an amused aside, and Heidi glared at her. 'She wants to go to London and do her own thing.'

'I'm afraid that's out of the question,' said Justin.

'But why? You never give me a good reason!' Heidi's face was slowly turning scarlet. Bryony sensed this was an argument that had taken place many times. 'Kurt will take a set of photographs of me to send round to the agencies. That's the way it's done. If they like me, they'll put me on their books.'

'Heidi, I hope you haven't been seeing Kurt van Arne against my wishes,' Justin said evenly. 'You know what I think of that young man. He's just using you.'

Heidi's chair scraped across the floor as she stood up abruptly.

'You . . . you just want to mess up my

life!' she cried dramatically. 'It's not fair!' And she rushed from the room and slammed the door.

Bryony was unsure whether to go after her but Justin lifted a hand and shook it slightly.

'Heidi has made a rather unsuitable friend,' he murmured.

Carla had continued eating as though nothing had happened. Now she gave Bryony a frosty smile.

'How did you hear that Justin needed a new secretary?' she asked. 'It seems strange that he gave you the job without an interview.'

'Time is pressing. I needed someone as soon as possible,' Justin put in, then smiled at Bryony. 'The notes are piling up, I'm afraid.'

Bryony turned to the other girl. 'My cousin Simon is a friend of Heidi's brother, Lance. I was looking for something different after the school where I taught history and drama closed down. Lance mentioned it.'

'I trust Lance's judgment,' Justin

added. 'If he thought Miss Redland would suit me, that was enough.'

'So you were a schoolma'am.' Carla raised her eyebrows in a supercilious way.

'Miss Redland doesn't look at all like a schoolma'am,' said Justin, 'except perhaps a very charming Victorian one.'

Bryony felt a little glow of triumph at Carla Willard's obvious annoyance. What made this girl think she could criticise and patronise her? Anyway, at least Justin had stood up for her. She attacked her roast lamb with relish.

Heidi didn't return to the dining-room and the meal continued with general conversation until they reached the coffee.

'I have some notes to complete tomorrow,' Justin told Bryony, 'then we can get down to some work. Perhaps it would be a good idea for you to familiarise yourself with the house and grounds. Heidi should be about to show you around.'

'I'll be quite all right on my own,'

said Bryony hastily. She could imagine Heidi's fury if Justin arranged her days for her. 'Actually, I strolled about a bit this afternoon. The flowers are wonderful.'

He smiled enthusiastically. 'I'm glad you think so. I confess they're one of my passions.'

'I wandered down the drive,' Bryony continued. 'It was so cool under the trees. The house is very isolated, isn't it? I couldn't see one building from the gateway.'

'The nearest houses are half a mile away,' said Carla, 'but the village is only a little farther on. It has a café, a few shops and an inn. Everything we need.'

'I met someone at the bottom of the drive,' Bryony commented. 'He seemed very nice.'

'Met someone?' Justin looked up sharply.

'Yes. A vet. He seemed very friendly.' She had a sudden feeling that it might be better not to go on, but the others were watching her and it was too late to draw back. 'We took a kitten to Nanny Flake.'

She saw Carla give Justin a quick glance. He stood up and threw a napkin on the table.

'I'll see you at dinner tomorrow, Miss Redland. Goodnight.' And with that he strode from the room.

There was a deep silence, Bewildered, Bryony looked across at Carla. The other girl finished her coffee without haste, replaced the cup in the saucer and stood up.

'You don't seem to have made a very good start, Miss Redland. Still glad you came? Mind you, he's not like that all the time.' And with that, she floated languidly from the room.

Bryony stared dejectedly into her coffee cup. Carla was right, she hadn't made a good start. What a fool she had been to mention Rowan. There was obviously a mystery there; she had sensed it earlier. So why had she said anything? Why hadn't she bided her time till she knew what was going on?

Settling In

Heidi, looking furtive, was waiting for Bryony as she left the dining-room. She was wearing jeans, a jacket and a woollen hat pulled down to cover her fair hair. She drew Bryony into an alcove and spoke in a low voice.

'Bryony, will you do something for me? If anyone asks, will you say we spent the evening together?'

'But why? Where are you going?'

'Never mind. I shan't be long.'

'But it's dark — it's late to be out on your own.' Bryony began to feel worried. 'Shall I come with you?'

'I shan't be on my own. I'm being picked up.' Heidi glanced at her watch. 'And I must hurry. Promise me you'll say we were together.'

'Well . . . ' Bryony felt she was getting out of her depth.

'Good.' Heidi took it as a 'yes.' 'I

won't be long.' She darted down a passage and was gone.

Bryony stood alone in the silent hall. It was as if she was the only person in the house. She could hardly go and look for Justin or Carla, and if she found them, there would be questions about Heidi. Worried, she retreated to her room. It was nine-thirty, far too early to go to bed. But what could she do?

Suddenly she made up her mind. Nanny Flake! 'Come and see me any time,' she had said. 'An ally,' Rowan had called her.

She was out of her evening clothes and into jeans and a sweater in no time. Emerging cautiously from her room, she crept along the corridor to the top of the stairs and peeped over. No-one in sight. She dreaded meeting Justin again. She sped up the opposite corridor and knocked on Nanny Flake's door.

The little old lady opened it, clutching the wriggling kitten.

'He wants to get down,' she said, 'but I daren't let him escape into the house. We'd never find him. Come in, come in. It's lovely to see you again.'

Bryony experienced a wonderful feeling of warmth as she entered the little sitting-room; not just the warmth of the fire but the warmth of Nanny Flake's welcome.

'Sit down. I'll make us both a nice cup of tea.'

She opened what looked like a floor-to-ceiling cupboard and revealed a tiny fitted kitchen.

Bryony got to her feet. 'May I look? Oh, it's perfect! I've never seen such a tiny kitchen.'

A miniature sink, a toaster, kettle and electric ring — all standing on a row of slim cupboards painted a sparkling red and white.

'It has everything I need,' said Nanny with satisfaction. 'All my meals come up from downstairs. This is really only for drinks and snacks.'

She placed red and white checked

cups on a matching tray, and Bryony smiled.

'You do love red, don't you?'

'It's bright. Bright and cheerful. I don't like to be miserable. If you're miserable, nobody comes to see you, and I love visitors.'

'Does Rowan come often?' asked Bryony, accepting a cup of tea.

'He pops in whenever he can. He's very busy.'

Nanny sat down and lifted the kitten on to her lap.

'Have you chosen a name for him?' Bryony asked.

'Yes. I'm going to call him Pickle because that's what he is.' As she held the little creature to her face and made loving noises to it, it put out a tiny pink tongue.

'How long have you lived in Greston Tower?' asked Bryony.

'Sixty years, come Christmas. I came here as nurserymaid in Mr Justin's fathers' day. When he and his brother went away to school I went to London as Nanny to another branch of the family.'

'Did you like living in London? It must have been very different from here.'

Nanny refilled their cups.

'I didn't like it at all. Noise and rush! I wanted to come back. And when Mr Justin was born, I did.'

'So you were Mr Sancerre's nanny?'

'Mr Justin is Mr Darke. Sancerre is just the name he uses for his books.'

Bryony frowned. 'But . . . Rowan is Mr Darke, too. Are they brothers?'

Nanny Flake looked at her curiously. 'Mr Rowan didn't explain anything to you?'

'No. And I wish he had. I'm afraid I've upset Mr Sancerre — I mean, Mr Darke. In fact, I really made him mad. And I don't know why. I told him that I'd met Rowan and that he had brought me to see you. I said he seemed very nice — but his reaction was most peculiar.'

Nanny Flake was silent for a long

while. The kitten snoozed in her lap. The only sound was the monotonous ticking of the clock. Bryony waited.

'I'd better tell you the whole story,' said Nanny at last. 'Somebody should.

'Mr Justin and Mr Rowan are cousins,' she began, 'born to two brothers almost on the same day. Mr Rowan's parents were vets, like him, but they worked abroad a lot. So he was sent to be brought up at Greston Tower and I was nanny to them both.

'They were lovely boys, no trouble at all.' She smiled and seemed to be looking at memories in the distant past. 'But everything changed when they fell in love with the same girl.'

'What happened?' asked Bryony, thoroughly absorbed by the story.

'Her name was Eleanor. The three of them had played together as children. The boys went away to school and when they came back, Eleanor was quite grown up. She was so beautiful. She had dark eyes and dark golden hair to her waist and she was so full of fun.

They both adored her.'

'And?' Bryony prompted.

'She chose Mr Rowan.'

'So he's married?' Bryony felt a stab of disappointment.

Nanny ignored the interruption.

'It was a tragedy. At the engagement party, Mr Justin drank too much and drove off into the night in Mr Rowan's new car. It was powerful, and he'd been drinking of course, and . . . ' She sighed. 'He crashed. He broke his right arm and his left wrist.'

'How dreadful!' Bryony breathed.

'He'd planned to be a concert pianist, but the accident put paid to that. Eventually he became a writer. And he never spoke to Rowan again. He blamed him for it all.'

'And Eleanor and Rowan?'

'They married. He became a vet.' Nanny's eyes grew sad. 'But two years later she died in childbirth. Their baby, too. It was a tragedy . . . '

'Poor man!' Bryony breathed. 'And he never married again?'

Nanny shook her head. 'He blames himself for her death, you see. Says that if she'd chosen Justin she would probably still be alive. So no, he never married again.'

'Poor man,' said Bryony again softly. 'But he still comes to Greston Tower to see you. Doesn't Justin object to that?'

'Oh yes! He doesn't want to see Mr Rowan or hear anything about him, so the visits have to be as quiet as possible. But yes, he comes to see me. I insist on it. I love them both equally. And this was his home.'

Bryony stared into the fire. There was so much to think about. She stood up, wanting to be alone for a while.

'Thank you for telling me, Nanny. I can be more guarded now when I speak to Mr Darke. *If* he still wants me to work for him.' She grimaced as she spoke.

Nanny patted her arm. 'Don't you worry — Justin's bark is worse than his bite. But if you'll take my advice, you'll stand up to him. Don't let him frighten you.'

★ ★ ★

As she returned along the corridor, Bryony looked out of the windows into the darkness. Where was Rowan now? She smiled to herself. Did she want to see him because she was attracted to him or because of his romantic story?

Whatever the reason, she'd better make sure Justin didn't suspect anything. Nanny's words came back to her: 'Stand up to him. Don't let him frighten you.' She would take that advice. Who was Justin to say who she should or should not be friendly with?

At the top of the stairs, she became aware of two figures in the hall below. Justin and Carla. He was just about to reach out and open the front door when Carla glanced up and saw Bryony. Deliberately, she pulled Justin close, twined her arms about his neck and kissed him. Over his shoulder, she looked up triumphantly at Bryony.

Before Justin could see her, Bryony hurried along the corridor to her own room.

So Carla Willard was demonstrating her claim? Well, let her, thought Bryony; it doesn't interest me in the least.

She was about to undress when there was a soft knock at the door. Opening it, she discovered Heidi, still in her outdoor clothes.

'Can I come in?' The girl glanced along the corridor then slipped into the room. 'No-one saw me go out so you won't need to fib for me.'

Bryony sighed. 'Heidi, I'm not happy about . . . '

'But you said we'd be friends!' she protested at once. 'What are friends for if not to support each other?'

'But don't you see, I'm in a position of trust?' Bryony appealed. 'If your guardian thought I was lying to him . . . '

'Oh — Justin!' Heidi scoffed, and sat

heavily on the bed.

'Is the person you went to see this Kurt van Arne? Mr Darke seemed very disapproving of him at dinner. Who is he?'

'I'd better tell you about it,' said Heidi.

Twice in one night I'm getting 'the story', thought Bryony. This job is proving very complicated and I haven't even started it yet!

'Kurt is a brilliant photographer,' Heidi began. 'He wants to do a feature on Greston Tower for a magazine — you know, home of the famous novelist and so on. But Justin won't allow it.'

'Why not?'

'Calls it invading his privacy,' said Heidi bitterly.

'Well, it would be,' said Bryony fairly. 'So where do you come in?'

'Kurt says that if I can persuade Justin to let him in, he'll take a fantastic set of photographs of me that will get me on to the books of a good model agency. He has contacts, too.'

Bryony looked at her, unsure what to say.

'Well? Don't you think I'd make a good model?' asked the younger girl. 'I'm tall and slim and I love clothes.'

'Mr Darke wants you to go to finishing school. Isn't that more sensible?' Bryony ventured. 'You're young to be alone in London. Perhaps you could try modelling later.'

'Finishing school,' Heidi said with disgust. 'I've had enough of school! I want to start my career. And besides, Kurt won't wait. He wants me to persuade Justin now. Perhaps you could . . . '

'No. Definitely not,' said Bryony at once. 'I'll have enough tightropes to walk as it is.'

'Tightropes? What d'you mean?'

Bryony told her about the meeting with Rowan and Justin's reaction to the incident.

Heidi smiled wryly. 'Rowan. Yes, that's a long-running feud.'

'Do you ever see him?' asked Bryony.

'Occasionally. About the village. We speak in passing but that's all. I have enough problems with Justin without adding that one. But Rowan's supposed to be very nice.'

She yawned and stretched her arms above her head.

'Well, I'm off to bed. And you must be tired, too. You've had quite an emotional introduction to Greston Tower and your new job.'

'Aren't you hungry? You've had no dinner,' Bryony pointed out.

The other girl grinned. 'Doesn't matter. A model has to watch her figure.'

As Bryony closed the door after her, she wondered whether being a secretary to Justin Sancerre would entail more problems than rewards.

But you wanted an interesting job, an adventure, she reminded herself. At least nothing about this job would be dull!

* ⋆ ⋆

The delicious smell of eggs and bacon greeted her as she entered the breakfast room next morning. No-one else was down yet, but there seemed no point in waiting so she helped herself to a liberal portion and sat down to enjoy it.

She had finished eating and was debating with herself whether to have toast and butter when Justin walked in.

'Ah, good morning, Miss Redland.' His voice was quiet and friendly. 'I hope you slept well.'

Should I apologise for last night, Bryony wondered. No, don't disturb his mood which, this morning, seemed a happy one.

'Wonderfully, thank you.'

She watched him covertly as he helped himself from the sideboard, until, turning quickly, he caught her looking at him.

'May I pour you some more coffee?'

'No, thank you,' she said hastily. 'I've

43

finished now. I'm going to do as you suggested and get to know the house and grounds.'

She pushed back her chair and stood up as she spoke. She must get away while he was still in a good mood.

Outside, she upbraided herself. What a coward! Was he a monster to be fled from? What about her resolution not to be frightened of him?

She took a deep breath. She would acclimatise herself to her employer's moods in her own good time. For now, she was going to enjoy the fresh morning air.

She was fascinated to find the garden near the house laid out as a series of rooms. Some featured a particular colour — she especially liked the white and silver one. Some emphasised one species of plant. One room was scented, another pebbled, with a fountain rising from a bowl in the centre. The only one she didn't like was the one with the collection of ugly stone gargoyles along the walls.

Beyond lay grassland and a small lake. To one side she could see a little wood with the roof of a summer-house in the shape of a pagoda rising above the trees.

The garden must have been a children's paradise, she thought. What a pity there were no children to enjoy it now.

Sinking down on to a wooden bench, she breathed in the scent of dozens of rose bushes around her. She supposed this was what would be called a rose arbour. How Aunt Margaret would love this garden, she mused. She was a keen gardener, but her own plot was average-sized, minute compared with this.

She heard the engine of a car start up. Was that Justin or Heidi? She hadn't seen the girl this morning.

Hearing it, she felt an urge to get into her own car and explore. The village wasn't far away. She could wander around for an hour; perhaps have a cup of coffee.

Buckley, the gardener, was outside the garages.

'Morning, miss. Want your car? I put it in the end one. I'll get it out for you.'

She waited, hearing with alarm a choking cough from the engine of her little car. It sounded very unhealthy. It was no surprise, then, when Buckley emerged on foot from the garage, shaking his head.

'Won't start, miss. I'll 'ave a look at 'er later on. I'm good with cars. And if I can't fix 'er, I'll get George from the garage in the village.'

He turned away and Bryony bit back her frustration. Well, she wouldn't be beaten; she would walk to the village.

When she went back to the house to collect a jacket, Justin was in the hall. He saw her before she could retreat.

'Ah, Miss Redland, are you sure you had enough breakfast?'

Bryony looked at him, startled. 'Yes, of course. Why?'

'It's just that you seemed to dart away as soon as I came in. I hope I didn't frighten you.'

Bryony felt childish and silly. She knew she shouldn't have run away like that. Whatever could she say?

Before she could answer, however, Justin took pity on her embarrassment.

'We'll have a chat another time,' he said. 'Enjoy the beautiful morning.' Then he was gone and Bryony could breathe again.

⋆ ⋆ ⋆

The morning was fresh and golden. She could see over the hedges to where fat white sheep cropped the grass, stopping now and then to give her a blank stare.

Unfortunately the road rose gently but relentlessly upwards. It wasn't a steep hill, especially in a car, but on foot it was tiring, and she had almost decided to turn back when the sound of a car slowing down behind her made her step on to the grass verge.

Instead of passing, however, the car stopped, a window was wound down and Rowan's face looked out.

'Are you walking for the good of your health or would you like a lift?'

'I'd love a lift, thanks!' She happily opened the passenger door and slid in. 'My car wouldn't start,' she explained. 'Buckley has promised to look at it.'

'He's good with cars.'

'So he said. I hope he is. I feel marooned without it.'

'Where d'you want to go? I'm at your disposal for an hour.'

'To the village, please. I'm curious to see what's there.'

He grinned. 'Not a lot. But it has a café which does surprisingly good coffee. Interested?'

'Very interested.'

The road led straight into the little village and Rowan parked in the square. An inn, the Red Lion, incongruously large for such a small village, faced an old Norman church across the square. There were three or four shops; Bryony noticed a general store and post office, a chemist and a fruit-and-flower shop.

Rowan led the way into the Copper Kettle tea-room and was greeted warmly by a rotund little woman in a smock. He ordered coffee and tea-cakes and they settled themselves at a table in the window.

Bryony looked around with interest. Copper jugs and pots on tables and shelves twinkled in the morning sunshine. The room looked crisp and clean.

'This village is quite unusual nowadays in that it is almost self-sufficient,' Rowan told her. 'We have the ubiquitous supermarket a few miles away, but it isn't essential to go there.'

'I love the black and white houses around the square.'

'They're a feature of most Worcestershire villages. Very picturesque.'

Their coffee arrived with generous-sized tea-cakes on a pottery plate. They smelt warm and spicy.

Mrs Paulet's smile at Bryony betrayed her curiosity.

'This is Miss Redland, Mr Darke's new secretary,' said Rowan, ignoring

Mrs Paulet's raised eyebrows. 'I'm sure she'll be a regular here. Mrs Paulet runs the best café in the village,' he confided to Bryony.

'Get along with you, Mr Darke, it's the *only* café in the village.' Mrs Paulet gave him an affectionate slap on the shoulder. 'Charm the birds off the trees he would,' she said to Bryony. 'I'm pleased to meet you, dear. You'll be welcome whenever you've time to call in. Now, eat your tea-cakes while they're warm.'

Bryony had just finished the last buttery crumb when she glanced out of the window and saw, leaning against a car opposite the café, a young man of about thirty whose golden hair blazed in the sunlight. He was talking to Heidi.

Rowan followed her gaze. 'That's Kurt van Arne,' he said. 'I gather Justin doesn't approve of the association.'

'You get your information from Nanny Flake, I suppose.'

'I do, and she doesn't miss a thing.' He poured them both another cup of coffee. 'What do you think of the delectable Carla Willard?' he asked.

'Delectable?'

'Well, she thinks so.' He grimaced. 'She has a very high opinion of herself. Mind you, she needs it; not many other people agree!'

'You mean she's not popular?'

He shook his head. 'She uses people. No-one is befriended just for themselves. But most people see through her.'

'Doesn't Justin?' she wondered.

He shrugged. 'Justin's no fool. They're using each other, if you ask me. She gets interesting outings and reflected glamour — famous author and so on — while he gets an attractive partner. But it's no more than that.'

'Heidi says Carla thinks Justin will marry her.'

Rowan looked doubtful. 'Justin has always said he won't marry. I think Carla's fooling herself.' He pointed across the road to a little lane at the side of the church. 'Her shop is up there — at the end of the lane.'

'Shop? Carla runs a shop?'

Rowan laughed at her incredulous expression.

'Not groceries or shoes. Carla calls it a studio. Cushions and lampshades. Frillies like that. Makes a lot of them herself. She's very good, very artistic, to be fair.'

'She more or less ignored me last night,' Bryony confided.

'She would,' said Rowan cheerfully. 'You have nothing to offer her and you could be a threat.'

'A threat?' Her eyes opened wide. 'How could I be a threat to her?'

'Because you're pretty and younger than she is. Justin might forget you're his secretary.'

She coloured. 'Don't be silly! Justin would never be interested in me.' She picked up her coffee cup to cover her confusion. 'I went to see Nanny last night,' she told him.

He looked keenly at her. 'Did you? So soon? Any special reason?'

She related the events of the evening.

'I felt miserable and confused,' she confessed. 'I couldn't think what to do, where to go. Then I remembered Nanny Flake.'

Rowan put his hand over hers on the table. 'I'm sorry I let you walk into that situation. But I didn't want to prejudice your opinion of Justin. He's a wonderful guy. We were once very close. But now . . .'

She nodded. 'Nanny told me.'

Rowan smiled ruefully and removed his hand. 'I've tried, goodness knows. But Justin can be so obstinate! He refuses to speak to me. Nanny told you the whole story, I suppose?'

She nodded. 'She said it was only fair I should know.'

'She's right. Nanny's generally right.'

The young couple outside were still chatting with animation and much laughter.

'If Justin sees them together there'll be fireworks,' Rowan commented. 'Heidi must like to live dangerously.'

Bryony thought it best not to mention Heidi's escapade of the night before.

She studied Kurt van Arne with interest. He was quite attractive, she decided, and wondered whether Heidi's interest was romantic as well as businesslike.

As they watched, Kurt leaned forward to give the girl a quick kiss on the cheek. Then he was in his car and away, while Heidi crossed the road and disappeared into the chemist shop.

'If you've finished, we can go now,' said Rowan. 'I didn't want to have to speak to them. I know Kurt reasonably well so I couldn't just have passed by. And it'll be best if you keep well away from him. Don't get involved with Heidi's schemes. You have to work with Justin, remember.'

'Thanks for the warning. But I don't intend to get involved.'

Rowan replaced his hand on hers. 'Seriously though, Bryony. I'll always be here if you need me. Don't feel again that you don't know what to do or where to go.' He reached into an inside pocket in his jacket and brought out a business card and handed it to her. 'My address and phone number. Don't be afraid to call me.'

She smiled her thanks and put the card in her bag. 'Thanks. Right — I'm ready. Shall we go?'

Outside, Rowan looked at her in consternation.

'We stayed there too long. You wanted to look round the village but I'm afraid I can't stay much longer — I have a clinic at twelve-thirty, and I want to drive you back first. It's a long walk.'

'Don't worry. As soon as my car's ready I can come again and look round. I must return to Greston Tower now in any case — I've been away long enough.'

Bryony was quiet on the short drive back, her mind occupied with the feud between the cousins. Wouldn't it be wonderful if she could be the one who brought them together? She had a daydream of Justin and Rowan shaking hands, even hugging each other, as she looked on with pride.

Rowan's voice jolted her into the present.

'When can I see you again?'

She looked across at the handsome face, so like Justin's. She had expected the question. They got on so well.

'Could I take you to dinner one night?' he asked.

'I'd like that, but I don't know what my plan of work will be yet. Justin hasn't discussed hours or conditions. He might like to work in the evenings. Can I ring you?'

'Of course. But don't leave it too long.'

He swung the car into the gateway of Greston Tower, and she began to thank him but he cut her short by reaching for her hand and pressing it to his lips.

'Goodbye, Bryony. I've enjoyed this morning.'

She opened the door and swung her legs out. As she did so, a red sports car sped down the drive and screeched to a stop next to them. With an exaggerated smile, Carla Willard waved from the driving seat then raced past them and up the lane.

Her eyes wide with alarm, Bryony turned back to Rowan, who gave her a rueful smile.

'Bad timing,' he said. 'Never mind, perhaps she'll forget to mention it!'

Bryony Makes An Enemy

Bryony walked slowly up the drive. Carla's appearance had spoilt an enjoyable morning. She wouldn't forget, Bryony was sure. She would mention it at the most embarrassing moment, probably during dinner. Then they would have another display of Justin's annoyance.

'Darn Carla Willard,' she said aloud.

Then a thought struck her. Why should it matter what Carla thought, or what Justin thought, for that matter? Why shouldn't she have a friend? If she saw Rowan in her own time, surely it was the business of no one but herself.

On that thought she emerged from the trees and marched determinedly across the drive to the house.

'Miss Redland!' The voice came from the garage side of the house. 'Miss Redland!'

Not Justin, she thought thankfully, and turned to see Buckley with a wide grin on his face.

'Told you I was good with cars, didn't I?'

'You've fixed it? Aren't you clever! It won't need to go to the garage then?'

'Nah. There's not much they can do that I can't.' His tone of complacency amused Bryony.

'What was wrong?'

He scratched his head. 'Needed coaxing,' he said vaguely. 'Gentle handling and coaxing.'

And with that mechanical explanation, she had to be content as he gave her a little salute and went back to the garden.

Smiling to herself, her good humour restored, Bryony entered the house. This time there was no one in the hall.

She went swiftly up the stairs to her room where she removed her jacket and looked at herself in the mirror. Her face was flushed, she noticed. She splashed it with cool water, renewed her lipstick and tidied her hair, then glanced at her watch. It was time for lunch.

The table in the dining-room was laid for one.

'Where is everyone?' she asked Mrs Buckley.

'Miss Heidi is out for the day and Mr Darke has a tray in the library. He's busy and doesn't want to stop for a proper meal.'

Well, at least I won't have to rush this time, thought Bryony with satisfaction, and thoroughly enjoyed her meal.

When she had finished, she wondered what to do. If only Justin had given her some work; idleness made the time pass slowly. And she was eager to make a start.

Wondering where Heidi had gone, she climbed the stairs to her room again and looked around rather aimlessly. What to do?

I know, she thought, I'll write to Aunt Margaret. She had nothing to tell about the job yet, but she could at least describe the house and its occupants

— though she decided to say nothing of the feud between Justin and Rowan, nor how intimidating she found Justin Darke.

'*I've spent some time with Justin's ward, Heidi,*' she wrote. '*She's younger than me but we get on well.*

'*I went to the village nearby today and had coffee with Justin's cousin, Rowan. I'll tell you more about him later. And don't get ideas, we're just friends!*'

She smiled to herself as she wrote this. Aunt Margaret was an incorrigible romantic.

She filled a page describing the house and grounds, then stopped for inspiration.

'*Tomorrow we're to start work properly,*' she wrote, '*and I'm looking forward to it.*'

She could think of nothing else to say. She sent her best wishes to them all, sealed the letter and took it downstairs. Mrs Buckley had told her that letters for the post could be left on the hall table and Buckley would take them to the post office later in the day.

At the bottom of the stairs she stopped, arrested by the tinkling notes of a piano nearby. It was a classical piece, but she couldn't remember the name. She followed the direction of the sound.

It took her down a passageway leading off the hall. She hadn't noticed it before. As she moved along, the music got louder.

The door to the room at the end of the passage was slightly ajar. The music was coming from there.

She stood listening, scarcely breathing, for a few minutes. The pianist's skill was impressive. Nanny's words came back to her: 'He'd planned to be a concert pianist.' Of course, it had to be Justin.

She listened, thrilled, to the cascade of notes, then, as it came to an end, she impulsively pushed open the door.

Justin was seated at a grand piano gazing into the garden. The room was beautiful, octagonal in shape, built out into the garden, with huge windows which seemed to invite the shrubs and flowers inside.

She must have made a sound because he spun round, and his face became a mask of fury.

'When I told you to get to know the house, Miss Redland, I did not invite you to spy on me.'

The attack was so sudden that Bryony jumped as if from a slap.

'What are you doing here?' he demanded. 'This music room is private. No one comes here without my express invitation.'

'I heard the music,' she faltered. 'It was so beautiful. The door was open. I came in without thinking. I'm sorry.'

'Do you never think first?' he asked coldly.

She struggled against an instinct to run from this overbearing man. But if she left the room, she knew she would run upstairs, pack her bags and leave for ever.

Instead, she advanced farther into the room and stood in front of him.

'Mr Darke — ' Her voice, at first tremulous, gained in strength as she went on, ' — you engaged me without an interview. It's not my fault if you don't like me. I was told nothing about your family before I came. How could I know you wouldn't approve of my acquaintance with Rowan? That's the real reason you're annoyed with me, isn't it?

'Well, let me assure you that Rowan told me nothing about you because he didn't want to influence me before I met you. He was being fair to you. And before anyone else feels obliged to tell you, I had coffee with him in the village this morning.'

Justin stood up, his face tense, a muscle twitching in his cheek. He looked very angry, but Bryony forced herself to stand her ground. In fact, she hadn't finished yet. She drew a deep breath.

'You don't have to be pleasant to me,

but I do want a normal working relationship with respect on both sides. If you want to change your mind, if you want me to leave, please tell me now. But I warn you, I won't stay to be bullied.'

He passed a hand over his face and they stood in silence, looking at each other. Then the tension in him seemed to ebb a little.

'Miss Redland, I apologise. I don't want you to leave. I didn't mean to bully you. Miss Gladstone, my secretary, has been with me for years. She understands me. I don't have to put on an act with her.'

'I don't want you to put on an act with *me*,' Bryony protested.

He took both her hands in his. 'I'm sorry. Can we start again?'

She looked down at the floor, hesitating.

'I was so thrilled to get this job. It's just the sort of project I want to be involved with.'

'Then — a new start?' he asked hopefully.

Bryony looked at the handsome face gazing so pleadingly at her. He still held her hands. It was unbelievable. Justin Sancerre, the famous writer, was begging her to take the fabulous job that she really wanted.

She smiled. 'A new start,' she agreed.

He tucked his hand under her elbow and led her towards the door.

'In that case, I'll show you the library and your special corner.'

★　★　★

They retraced her steps to the hall where Justin opened a heavy door and ushered her inside.

'Goodness, I've never seen so many books! Have you read them all?' she asked impulsively.

He laughed. 'Not quite, but I started young so I have read quite a few.'

Except for the windows, the room was completely lined with bookshelves. Glass-fronted cases contained sets of volumes in uniform bindings. Some appeared very old. Open shelves held an eclectic collection; old books in battered covers, new ones in brightly-coloured dust covers, small books, large books, thick and thin, they climbed the walls almost to the ceiling.

'How do you reach the very top shelves?' she wondered.

He pointed to the corner. 'Special library ladders. But you must be very careful when you use them.'

'How many books are there?' She was still gazing around in wonder.

He shrugged. 'I don't think anyone has ever counted. But, of course, I'm still adding to them. Here's your corner.' He walked over to a desk to the right of the huge stone fireplace. 'It's very snug in winter. We have log fires.'

'Where do you write?' she wondered.

He tapped the huge oak table in the centre of the room, its top pitted and worn.

'Here sometimes, but I also have a special place. Come and see.'

He opened a door which she hadn't

noticed before, faced with shelves of books and fitting snugly into a wall of books so that it was completely camouflaged.

'A secret door!' she said delightedly.

She followed him into a small room containing little more than a table and a swivel chair.

'No windows.' He waved a hand. 'Nothing to distract me. This is where I do most of my writing and where I must never be disturbed — ' he looked at her solemnly ' — unless there's a fire.'

And I don't think he's joking, thought Bryony.

They returned to the library where Justin lifted a box file from a shelf and opened it.

'These might interest you.' He took some packets of letters, tied with blue tapes, from the file. 'Have you noticed the portrait of the Indian girl in the hall?'

'Yes. Heidi said she's part of a family mystery.'

'These letters refer to her,' said Justin. 'Let's go and look at her portrait.'

They stood before the painting in its heavy gold frame. The girl was very beautiful, with an emerald silk shawl edged with gold almost covering the jet black hair. Her features were perfect. Long lashes fringed the eyes which were lowered modestly. Her brown skin was powdered with gold and gold jewellery shone in her ears and round her smooth throat.

Bryony gazed in fascination at one piece, a flower pendant set with tiny emeralds. It was exquisite.

'Isn't she lovely? Who is she?'

'Sir Andrew Darke had tea estates in India,' Justin explained. 'He travelled back and forth from England to India every year. After one trip, he brought back this lovely girl. Her name was Anila.

'Her father had been one of his managers until he was mauled to death by a tiger. The man's wife had several daughters to marry off, so Sir Andrew offered to adopt Anila, bring her to England and find her a husband.'

'What on earth did Sir Andrew's wife think?' asked Bryony. 'The girl was very beautiful. Wasn't she jealous?'

'There's no record of that,' he said, smiling again. 'But the letters I've put out for you record what impression she made on the neighbourhood. One of Sir Andrew's sisters was unmarried and lived here in the family home. She was a great letter writer, fortunately for us, and wrote often to her sisters and friends. These letters have been collected together and we get a picture of the minor celebrity she became in the neighbourhood when she went out to local dinners and parties in her beautiful saris and jewels.'

'What became of her? Did she find a husband?'

'No. Tragically she died. Our winters were too cold for her. She caught pneumonia just six months after coming to England.'

'Poor girl!' Bryony studied the lovely face. 'What a sad story.'

They returned to the library.

'Have you a portrait of Sir Andrew?' asked Bryony.

He pointed to a huge full-length oil painting between the two central windows.

'There he is. It's very true to life, I believe.'

Bryony walked across to stand in front of the massive portrait. The eyes, with their quizzical expression, stared out at her from under Justin's straight brows. In fact, remove the sideburns and the whiskers and it could be a portrait of Justin himself.

She remained in front of it for several minutes, almost mesmerised by the image.

'What are you thinking?' Justin asked.

She turned. 'I was thinking that he looks exactly like you,' she told him shyly.

He nodded. 'And my father and my

grandfather. The family likeness is carried down through the generations.'

'He looks very determined,' she observed.

'He was,' he agreed. 'Anything he set his mind to, he achieved. He was very young when he built this house, but later he built a theatre in Bardley, five miles away.'

'A theatre! Is it still there?'

'Oh yes. But I believe it flourishes mainly as an amateur venture. The family has no link with it now. In the nineteenth century it was very popular, though. Great-grandmama was an actress there, in fact.'

She raised her eyebrows. 'Sir Andrew married an actress? That was very daring for those days, wasn't it?'

'Mm, not so unusual. It wasn't unknown for actresses to marry into noble families and become titled. But in this quiet country area it did cause a slight scandal. Fortunately she proved an excellent wife and bore him three sons. The eldest was my grandfather.'

'And when did Sir Andrew die?'

'In nineteen forty-two, during the Second World War. He was an old man then, but active to the end, still making alterations to the house and grounds and visiting his theatre up to the last.

'He received his knighthood very late in life. He spent a lot of his money sponsoring shows at the theatre. It was wartime and he felt the ordinary people and soldiers on leave — needed to be cheered up. They were very popular.'

'And his wife?'

'She died before the war started.'

'You know a lot about him already,' Bryony observed. 'I'm beginning to see him as a man, not just a portrait.'

'What sort of man?' asked Justin with interest.

She thought for a moment.

'Well, of course, I only know what you've told me, but he seems to have been a thoughtful, caring man. I suppose if he made a lot of money as a businessman, he must have been clever, perhaps even ruthless, but I'd say he certainly had a kind, unselfish side to his nature.'

'It seems we're going to be thinking along the same lines,' he said with approval. 'Now, would you like to glance at those letters while I check some notes?'

He put the box file on her desk and pulled out the chair for her, then bent over her to open the box, and for a moment his whole presence seemed to enfold her. Bryony held her breath.

Then a telephone rang somewhere nearby and the spell was broken.

'I may see you at dinner tonight,' he said. 'We'll start work properly tomorrow,' and he disappeared behind his book-lined door.

Bryony gave a sigh of satisfaction and untied the tape around the first bundle of letters. At last she was doing something she knew she would enjoy.

She extracted the first letter from its envelope. It was dated 8th September, 1891. She peered at the spidery writing.

'*My dearest sister,*' she read. '*We are*

all very happy to know that you are settled in your new home.'

Unbidden, Bryony's eyes left the letter and went to those of the portrait; Justin's eyes with their fascinating downward slant and level brows. And Rowan's eyes, too, she reminded herself. But this time it was Justin's face which remained with her.

She mentally shook herself and returned to the letter.

'Our brother's Indian girl is still causing great interest,' she read. 'On Friday we took her to an evening party at the home of Mr and Mrs Randall. You remember them, I am sure. Mr Jesmond, the curate, was there and seemed unsure how to treat Anila. Poor man, he has spent months encouraging the children of the parish to donate their half-pennies to the relief of their brown brothers across the sea, and now he is faced with a brown sister wearing beautiful clothes and jewellery and meeting him as an equal. It has really confused the poor man.'

Bryony smiled to herself. It seemed that Sir Andrew's sister had a pronounced sense of humour. The letters would be most enjoyable to read. She took another from the bundle.

For an hour she worked through the letters, learning a great deal about life in Greston Tower at the end of the nineteenth century. It had been an altogether more bustling place then. The house had been filled with servants, many gardeners tended the extensive grounds and there had been a constant flow of relatives and visitors.

What a contrast with today. Bryony listened. Not a sound could be heard.

The library door opened slightly and Carla Willard looked in. Her expression, which had been playful, changed when she saw Bryony.

'Still here?' she drawled as she came into the room. 'I thought you'd been frightened away. You must be braver than you look.'

Bryony ignored her and, choosing another letter, began to study it.

'Justin can be very fierce, you know.' Carla seated herself at the end of the long table. 'Do you think you can tame him?'

'I don't think . . . ' began Bryony, but Carla wasn't interested

'Some men are tigers on the outside,' she continued, 'but inside, they're just pussy cats. Justin isn't one of those. He's all tiger.'

Bryony glanced at the door in the bookshelves. Thank goodness it was tightly closed. It would be very embarrassing if Justin could hear Carla.

'We're alike, Justin and I,' said Carla. 'We both like to fight and to dominate. That's why we're so well-suited. We find life exciting. Justin could never be happy with a meek and mild yes-woman.'

'Please,' said Bryony, wondering how to get rid of her. 'I have work to do.'

'Where *is* Justin?' Carla looked round the room. 'Never mind, I'll catch him later. I want him to take me out to dinner. Tell him to ring me,' she added as she sauntered from the room, leaving the door wide open.

A few minutes later, Bryony heard the sports car roar past the window and down the drive. She glanced towards Justin's door. It was still closed.

She crossed to close the door Carla had left gaping — and when she returned to her desk, Justin was standing in the doorway of his writing room.

'Miss Willard was here . . . ' Bryony began.

'I heard her,' Justin broke in shortly. 'Miss Willard has a penetrating voice and a vivid imagination. And I'm afraid I have rather acute hearing.'

She turned away, embarrassed when she thought of Carla's comments.

'Her number is on the phone pad,' Justin told her. 'Will you please phone her and say I have another engagement this evening?'

'But she was definite . . . '

'Just tell her that.' He returned to his room, annoyance plain on his face.

Bryony looked nervously at the telephone. She flicked the pad to the letter W and selected Carla's number. Please let her not be home yet, she willed as she dialled.

'Carla Willard,' came the superior voice at the other end.

'This is Bryony Redland. I have a message for you from Mr Darke. He has a previous engagement and will be unable to take you to dinner tonight.'

There was a pause, then, 'You little cat!' Carla spat out. 'What did you tell him?'

'I didn't have to tell him anything.' Bryony forced her voice to remain steady. 'Mr Darke has acute hearing. He heard our conversation from his writing room. Is there any message?'

'Tell him . . . tell him . . . Oh, get lost!' snapped Carla.

As Bryony replaced the telephone, she couldn't repress a smile of triumph. But at the same time she knew she had made a dangerous enemy.

A Dilemma For Bryony

Justin crossed the hall as Bryony and Heidi were entering the dining-room.

'If anyone wants me, I'm dining at The Mill. I want to see how Guy's getting on with his alterations.' He gave a slight wave and disappeared through the front door.

'The mill?' Bryony looked inquiringly at Heidi as they settled themselves at the table.

'Guy Vernon is turning the old mill in the village into a restaurant,' she explained. 'He's a friend of Justin's.'

Bryony enjoyed her meals alone with Heidi. There was no need to change into anything dressy, and she and the younger girl were able to chat without restraint.

'I need to buy some clothes,' Bryony told her. 'Is there anywhere other than the village?'

'Bardley's our nearest town,' said Heidi. 'They have a department store and quite a few fashion shops.'

'Bardley?' The name was familiar, and she suddenly remembered why. 'Where Sir Andrew Darke built his theatre?'

'Yes. It's quite near. D'you want to try the shops there?'

'Please. And I'd so like to see the theatre, too. Do you often go there?'

'I've never been,' Heidi admitted. 'I'm not really a theatre person. There are two cinemas, though. They're more in my line.'

'Oh.' Bryony was disappointed. The theatre was in her blood. She had hoped that she and Heidi might pay a few visits.

'Perhaps Justin would take you,' the girl suggested mischievously. 'In the cause of research, of course.'

Bryony said nothing as she concentrated on checking her fish for bones, but her thoughts were whirling. What if Justin suggested a theatre visit? In the cause of research, of course. Or Rowan . . .

'Would you like to go out this evening?' Heidi asked suddenly. 'You haven't been anywhere since you arrived.'

Bryony hadn't mentioned her trip to the village. She felt guilty at having observed Heidi with Kurt. Anyway, coffee in a tiny village café hardly counted as an outing.

'Out where?'

'There's a place I'm dying to visit about ten miles away,' said Heidi. 'It has a restaurant — of course, we shan't need that — and a bar and a disco. It's quite a big place.'

'Well — yes, it might be fun.'

'We'll go to the disco for a few hours,' said Heidi. 'Jeans and a top will do.'

The two girls ran upstairs to change and in fifteen minutes were in Heidi's car and turning from the drive into the lane.

Heidi was a good driver, but fast, and

Bryony was relieved when they turned into the car park of the Cherrytrees.

Bryony had never been one for discos, and she found it very loud and very bright, but Heidi's face glowed with excitement.

'Of course, it's best to be in a party,' she yelled above the noise, 'but I don't know many people around here. That's the disadvantage of going to a boarding school. My friends live all over the country.'

They accepted a few invitations to dance, but mostly bobbed around together on the fringes of the crowd. Bryony found herself enjoying it: she had been sitting around too much over the last few days.

At half-past ten, she suggested returning to Greston Tower. Heidi's face fell.

'Already? But it's not late,' she protested.

'We shan't be back till well after eleven,' Bryony pointed out.

Reluctantly Heidi got to her feet.

'I suppose you're right. We don't want to arrive after Mrs Buckley has locked up.'

They made their way through the crush to the door.

'My scarf!' said Heidi. 'I must have left it on my seat. I'll just go back and get it.'

'OK — I'll wait for you in the foyer.'

Bryony pushed open the heavy door and stepped into the foyer. Two men were just entering the bar on her right. One of them was Justin.

Guiltily she glanced behind her. There was no sign of Heidi.

He came across towards her.

'Miss Redland — I hope you're enjoying yourself.'

She felt herself colour up.

'Yes, thank you. We're just leaving. Perhaps I should explain . . . ' Why did she feel confused, even guilty? Was it the thought that he wouldn't expect her to bring Heidi to a place like this? But it had been Heidi's suggestion!

He held up his hand. 'No explanations necessary.' His voice was cool. 'What you do and who you do it with in your own time are no concern of mine. I'll see you tomorrow. Goodnight.'

He followed the other man into the bar and Bryony was left wondering what had happened to Heidi.

Then she saw her outside, beckoning furiously. She had left by another door.

'That was a near squeak,' she giggled when Bryony joined her. 'You didn't mention me, did you?'

'No. I think he thought I was with Rowan. I don't know anyone else here. He obviously didn't think of you.' They were walking towards the car, but she suddenly stopped and looked at Heidi. 'Would he have minded if he'd known you were here?'

'Minded? I'll say! He'd have gone nuts! That's why you mustn't tell him. Come on, the car's just over there.'

Bryony remained where she was and Heidi turned back inquiringly.

'Heidi, this is wrong. I didn't dream

that he'd be annoyed if you came here.'

Heidi looked impatient. 'For goodness sake, don't be such a goody-goody! Live a little! If I don't care, why should you?'

'Because he's my employer. He trusts me,' Bryony pointed out reasonably. 'Please, Heidi, don't get me into trouble. I don't want to lose this job. If I can't trust you, how can we be friends?'

'Well, we won't tell him and then neither of us can get into trouble,' Heidi said silkily, linking her arm through Bryony's and leading her towards the car. 'Anyway, it hasn't got *such* a bad reputation.'

Bryony groaned. 'Bad reputation?'

'A few of the people who go there are a bit wild, but we probably won't go again, so let's forget it.'

She opened the car doors and they got in, and as she turned the key and the car started, she glanced at Bryony.

'I wonder what Justin was doing there? Was he with Carla?'

'No — some guy.'

'Probably Guy Vernon,' Heidi decided. 'Carla won't be pleased if she finds out. She's beginning to think she should go everywhere with Justin.'

'Carla's not in favour at the moment,' Bryony commented, and related the incident in the library.

Heidi chortled with glee. 'How wonderful! How are the mighty fallen. But she won't like you any better because of it.'

'I know.' Bryony watched the trees flashing past in the headlights. 'I've already realised that.'

★   ★   ★

Wanting to create a good impression on her first working day, Bryony was at her desk at five minutes to nine. Keep office hours, she thought to herself, good for discipline.

But the library was empty. Justin wasn't there to appreciate her good start. She sat at her desk and read the notes he had left.

'*Please type these notes and file the reference cards in the appropriate drawers in my room,*' she read.

The pile of notes was high and would keep her busy all morning. She switched on the computer and got started.

She worked solidly and was surprised to discover that it was eleven o'clock when Mrs Buckley came in with a tray. She stretched her arms above her head.

'Busy?' asked Mrs Buckley.

'Yes. But I prefer it. Time drags when you're not.'

She poured herself a cup of coffee and drank it looking out of the window. Where was Justin, she wondered.

She watched Buckley carefully weeding a flower border. Then Mrs Buckley joined him and after a few words, they both went round the side of the house. Their coffee time too, she thought.

She was turning away from the window when she saw Heidi's tiny car shoot from the garage area and down the drive. Where was she off to? Not Kurt again! But perhaps she had another friend nearby, a more suitable friend. But Bryony knew this was unlikely.

The ring of the telephone took her away from the window.

'This is Carla Willard,' drawled a voice when she picked up the receiver. 'I want to speak to Mr Darke.'

'I'm afraid he's out,' said Bryony shortly.

There was a pause.

'When will he be back?'

'I can't say,' said Bryony.

'Can't or won't?' Carla snapped. 'It hasn't taken you long to behave like the dragon guarding the gate, has it? But if I want to speak to Mr Darke, I shall speak to him.'

'Of course. I'll tell him you rang.' Bryony's voice was expressionless which seemed to infuriate the other woman.

'Don't get ideas above your position,' she said icily. 'You're only a temporary help, remember, and I'll still be here long after you've gone,' and on that venomous note she slammed down the receiver.

Shaken, but hoping she hadn't shown it, Bryony hung up. It hadn't taken Carla long to show her feelings.

Deciding against another cup of coffee, for it was cold by now, she settled again to her typing. She was enjoying the task; Justin seemed to have uncovered an amazing amount of information about Sir Andrew Darke. The notes referred to diaries and log books, account books and estate maps. She would ask him if she might see them.

To rest her eyes from the bright computer screen, she took the pile of reference cards to Justin's writing-room. It didn't take long to file them in the drawers, and she was about to leave the room when she paused and looked around. Just think, this was where he had dreamed up all those novels she had enjoyed so much.

She sat in his huge leather chair and gently swung herself to and fro. The air was faintly scented with his aftershave. Who would have believed, just a few weeks ago, that she would be in Justin Sancerre's writing-room, sitting in his chair . . . Suddenly she sprang to her feet. What if he came in and found her?

Like a naughty schoolgirl caught sitting in the headmistress's chair, she scuttled out, closed the door and settled herself again behind her computer.

'*Sir Andrew Darke was born in 1862,*' she read. '*He was the only boy in a family of six children and educated at home by his father and a succession of tutors.*'

Bryony imagined the house ringing with the happy sound of children's voices; laughter in the gardens, singing in the drawing-room. She contrasted it with the silence of the house nowadays. Then she thought of Justin and his piano. At least there was still music, even if there wasn't much laughter.

She turned again to the notes.

'*He was strongly influenced by his father's brother, an explorer in Africa. As soon as he was old enough, he joined his uncle on some of the expeditions. Then he organised his own trips, frequently visiting India.*'

Now we're coming to the Indian girl, she thought. She must have sat in this very room, perhaps looking out of the window at the cold, wet English winter and longing for her own sunny climate and her family. Poor Anila.

I'd better stop day-dreaming, she admonished herself, or these notes won't be finished today.

She was hard at work again when she heard Justin's footsteps in the corridor. She felt a sudden twinge of apprehension. What if he had discovered Heidi was her companion at the Cherrytrees? Please don't let him mention it, she prayed, as the door opened.

'Good morning, Miss Redland.' His voice was cheerful. He dumped a pile of books at the end of the table. 'I've just collected these from the public library. Hard at work?'

'Nearly finished,' she said. 'And I've filed the cards.'

'Good.' He came behind her and looked over her shoulder. 'I see you've been busy. Do you think it's warm enough to sit in the garden?' he added.

She looked up at him in surprise.

'It's a lovely day,' he went on. 'I'll ask Mrs Buckley to bring us out some sandwiches and coffee and we'll have lunch while we talk. I want to chat about Heidi.'

He left the room. Chat about Heidi? Well, at least he looked quite cheerful about it, she thought thankfully, so it can't be anything to do with last night.

★   ★   ★

It was a beautiful early autumn day and she breathed the fresh, flower-scented air with pleasure. They strolled around the paths between the flower beds and shrubs, Justin pointing out his favourite plants and asking her opinion in a most flattering way.

At first she was too nervous to say much, feeling she had nothing of value to contribute, but he was polite and patient and seemed at pains to draw her out.

She studied his face as he bent over a particularly beautiful rose, and thought with a pang how handsome he was. To be so attractive and have had such a sad love life. And to waste himself on Carla Willard . . .

He turned and caught her studying him. Their eyes met and Bryony felt the colour rise in her cheeks.

She was freed from the embarrassing moment by the appearance of Mrs Buckley with a tray. Justin moved to take it from her, and by the time they were seated in the little rose arbour, Bryony had regained her composure.

'This was my mother's favourite place in the garden,' he told her. 'I've kept it just as she had it. Always the same roses.'

'You love roses, don't you?' she ventured.

'I love all flowers, but roses are my favourites. And I'm so lucky with Buckley, he's a superb gardener.'

'And good with cars.'

He smiled. 'You've discovered that.'

They ate in companionable silence. Bryony thought she had never been in such a peaceful place. The drone of the bees in the nearby flowers and the warmth of the sun on her upturned face almost sent her to sleep, so that she started when Justin spoke to her.

'If you've finished, perhaps we can discuss my ward? I think you've become friends in the short time you've been here.'

She nodded. 'We get on very well.'

'I'm glad. Heidi's a problem to me, I don't mind admitting. I'm not very good with teenagers — or discipline. Heidi needs a woman's guidance and there really isn't anyone.'

'Well, of course, I'll do anything I can to help,' she said doubtfully, 'but I'm only five years older than her. Hardly a mother figure.' She gave a little laugh.

'But you're sensible,' said Justin. 'You travelled a lot with your father and you've worked in a school. You've had quite a wide experience of life in a short time.' He smiled. 'Heidi wouldn't listen to an older person, I'm sure.'

She didn't have to ask what the problem was; it had to be Kurt van Arne.

Justin sighed. 'I love Heidi very much,' he said. 'When she was little, she loved me. Now I feel she hates me at times.' He paused. Bryony waited.

'She has this ridiculous idea of going to London and becoming a model, and that friend of hers, Kurt van Arne, doesn't help. She can't see that he's only pretending to be her friend to gain entry to Greston Tower for his own ends.'

'He has promised to take a set of photographs to help her career,' she reminded him.

'Help her career!' he said with

disgust. 'It's sheer unadulterated bribery, but she can't see it.'

'You really want her to go to finishing school?' she asked.

'Only because I think she'd enjoy it. If she has an alternative suggestion — a sensible one — I'll discuss it. But I'll never agree to her going off to London to pursue such an unstable career.'

'Has she any other interests you could encourage?' she wondered.

'That's where you can help, if you will. Get her to confide in you. Try to find out if there's anything else she'd like to do.'

'I'll feel like a spy,' said Bryony unhappily.

'But you'll be helping her.' He gazed at her with a serious expression. 'Together we can sort out a good future for her, not one which could put her in danger from starvation diets and goodness knows what else.'

He sat back in his chair, folded his arms and looked at her.

'I'm sorry, Miss Redland, you didn't

expect this when I engaged you as a secretary. Perhaps I'm asking too much. As you say, you're only five years older than Heidi.'

Bryony wasn't sure how to phrase her reply. She wanted to keep Heidi's friendship, but she was flattered that Justin had asked her to help him.

'I'll do my best,' she said at last, 'but Heidi and I have already become friends and I don't want to jeopardise that friendship.'

'Of course not. She needs a friend.'

'If I can help without upsetting her . . . '

'That's all I ask. If you can discourage her friendship with that man and suggest an alternative career, you'll have achieved more than I ask.' He stood up. 'I'm going in to start some work, but, please, take another hour and I'll see you later.'

Bryony leaned back and turned her face to the sun. Just five minutes, she told herself.

She mused on her conversation with

Justin. It was easy for him to say, 'discourage her friendship with that man.' But Heidi was besotted with Kurt and saw him and his photographs as her passport to an exciting new life.

I'll have to play it by ear, she thought. Grasp the opportunity when it arises. Justin can't expect miracles.

Reluctantly she left the sun and the scented garden and carried the tray of empty dishes towards the house.

⋆　⋆　⋆

In her bedroom, a large suitcase sat reproachfully in front of the wardrobe. Might as well empty it now, she thought. There's time before I go back to the library.

It was a luxury to have so much wardrobe space. Her bedroom at Aunt Margaret's was quite small.

She hung dresses and skirts, draped trousers over hangers and placed shoes in pairs at the bottom. She was just fastening the empty case when there was a knock at the door. In the corridor was a flushed and excited Heidi.

'Can I come in or are you busy? I've got something to show you.'

'Come in, I've just finished.'

Heidi shrugged off her coat and perched on the edge of Bryony's bed. With a triumphant smile, she slid a pile of glossy photographs from an envelope and lined them up on the bedcover.

'There! What d'you think?'

Bryony stood beside her and studied the photographs. She had to admit they were excellent. Heidi, in a variety of clothes and poses, showed an undoubted talent for modelling.

'What do you think?' the girl asked again. 'Of course, these are just trial shots. He'll do the proper ones later on.'

'Well ... of course, they're very good. You look fabulous. But ... '

'But what?' Heidi was indignant.

'I can't help thinking that Justin ... '

The girl looked annoyed. 'Why bring

him up? Can't you just look at the photographs and give me an honest opinion?'

'I've given you my opinion,' Bryony pointed out reasonably. 'You look fabulous. But you can't leave Justin out of it. He's your guardian. And what good are these if you can't show them to him?'

'I daren't show them,' she confessed.

'Because of Kurt van Arne?'

'It's so unfair.' Heidi gathered the photographs together. 'These *prove* that I could be a model.'

'I don't think Justin doubts your ability, but he feels you're too young to live in London on your own. And the modelling profession has a lot of dangers for someone who is young and unused to that sort of life.'

Heidi sat with a rebellious pout, nursing her packet of photographs.

A sudden thought struck Bryony.

'You have an aunt in London, haven't you? Could you live with her?'

Heidi shook her head. 'She's elderly

and not well. She couldn't be bothered with me.'

'What's in this for Kurt?' Bryony asked curiously.

Heidi shot her a glance. 'Nothing. He's doing it out of friendship.'

Bryony raised a sceptical eyebrow. 'I hardly think so. Isn't he trying to get you to persuade Justin to let him take photographs of Greston Tower?'

Heidi said nothing.

'Justin doesn't trust him, and with good reason I should think,' Bryony added unwisely.

Heidi's eyes flashed. 'What do you know about it? You've only been here a few days. You've never even met Kurt. All you know is what Justin has told you.'

Bryony had to admit the truth of that. But Heidi was only seventeen and Kurt a smooth and experienced older man. She looked at Heidi's mutinous face and wondered what to say next.

'You said we'd be friends,' Heidi stormed. 'But you can't be my friend if you side with Justin.' She stood up and glared at her. 'From now on you're Justin's secretary, that's all.' She snatched up her coat and stalked from the room, slamming the door behind her.

I've been here less than a week and already I've made two enemies, Bryony thought. What a start to a new career!

Disconsolately she applied fresh lipstick and went downstairs. Should I tell Justin, she wondered, or wait for an opportunity to put things right with Heidi?

Still undecided, she entered the library to find it empty, and several letters on her desk waiting to be typed. Decision postponed, she thought thankfully.

The feeling of disappointment and sadness hung over her all afternoon. She wished the conversation with Heidi hadn't taken place; that she hadn't promised to help Justin. But the afternoon's work couldn't be undone. She had done nothing for Justin and had lost Heidi's friendship.

Thoroughly miserable, she gazed unseeing through the window. The library door was slightly open and out of the corner of her eye she saw a tiny tortoiseshell shape dart across the room and jump up at the heavy tassel on the curtain tie-back.

'Pickle!' Bryony was out of her chair and across the room. The little kitten danced away and ran behind the other curtain. Closing the door so that he shouldn't escape, she crept towards his hiding place, then dropped to her knees and peeped behind the heavy drape.

'Is this what you're looking for?'

Turning her head, she saw Justin standing behind her, Pickle cradled in his hands. He had been in his writing-room and heard the commotion.

Feeling rather silly, she got to her feet, brushing the knees of her trousers.

'He must have escaped,' she explained. 'He shouldn't be down here.'

Justin held up the kitten and studied his little face.

'D'you know, he has the same colouring as you,' he said, 'tortoiseshell hair and green eyes. Does he belong to you?'

'No, he's Nanny Flake's new kitten. His name's Pickle.'

'That sounds appropriate. Would you like to take him home? I think we've finished for this afternoon.'

★   ★   ★

Thankfully she escaped and carried the kitten upstairs. How strange that Justin should comment on her colouring in almost the same way as Rowan.

She knocked on Nanny Flake's door and was almost unsurprised to find it opened by Rowan. This was an afternoon of incidents.

'I was just leaving,' he said. 'I wondered whether I might see you but didn't think it likely.'

Bryony handed Pickle to Nanny

Flake who began to scold him gently and was rewarded with a lick of his tiny tongue. She barely noticed them leave.

'Can I walk down to your car with you?' Bryony asked. 'It's so nice to see a friendly face.'

Rowan raised an inquiring eyebrow. 'Problems with Justin?' he ventured as they crossed the drive to the shrubbery.

'Oh, no, he's been fine. We're getting on quite well really. No, it's Heidi. I dared to criticise Kurt.'

'She'll forget it,' said Rowan dismissively. 'She needs you. Don't worry.' He linked his arm with hers and they walked in friendly silence to the car at the bottom of the drive.

'Are you free tomorrow evening?' he asked as he opened the door.

'Well, yes, I'm sure I am.'

'Then I'll call for you at eight. It's a party but nothing grand. I can introduce you to a few people. Your world is too small here. Do you good to get out.' He blew her a kiss and was off.

Bryony watched the car go out of

sight. She was pleased to be going out with Rowan but couldn't help a slight pang of disappointment. How much better if their outing was to be a romantic meal for two.

An Overheard
Conversation . . .

Rowan's party was a disappointment. Parties meant people, of course, but there were so many and he seemed to know them all.

Bryony was surprised right from the first moment when they drew up in the car park of a bright, modern hotel. 'Party' to her meant a house, not a hotel.

'Whose party is it?' she asked as they crossed the car park to the entrance.

'Oh, it isn't a private one,' he said. 'It's the Young Farmers. They love the excuse of a get-together to have a drink and a laugh. Must be something to do with all those hours spent in fields with only sheep and cows for company!'

They were grabbed as soon as they entered and invited to sit with Andy, another vet, and his wife, Fiona.

'This is Justin's new secretary, Bryony,' said Rowan, introducing her.

'Justin's new secretary?' Fiona looked at them both curiously.

'Shall we dance?' Rowan pulled Bryony to her feet, ending any more questions.

'Sorry,' he said as they edged into the crowd on the dance floor. 'There are even more people here than usual. It must be daunting for you, knowing no one.'

Daunting and disappointing, she thought. She had hoped for a chance to talk with him, to get to know him better, but this evening wasn't going to be the time.

'We could leave early and go somewhere else,' he offered.

'No, of course not. I'm enjoying it. And I love dancing.' She was enjoying his arms around her and the sensuous feeling of their bodies moving together to a soft, romantic tune.

'I love your dress,' he said. 'It

matches your eyes.'

There would be other opportunities to talk, she thought. Perhaps not so many chances to be held like this. She smiled up at him and he pulled her closer.

★　★　★

In the days following the party, Bryony found life very quiet. She worked each day in the library, either alone or with Justin.

He had spread the original architect's plans of Greston Tower on the big centre table and together they would pore over it, searching for original features and alterations. She felt proud when she was first to spot an elusive feature or made an intelligent comment. His approval became very important to her.

It was intriguing work, and she felt sorry whenever he left her to go to his writing-room and she had to return to the mundane tasks of typing and filing.

At home, she had exercised regularly at the local gym. Now the garden became her fitness area. Every lunchtime, and sometimes before breakfast, she walked to the lake and back as many times as she could, trying to beat the previous day's count, and was pleased that her weight remained constant despite Mrs Buckley's delicious food!

Heidi treated her with remote politeness, and if Justin noticed the coolness between the girls, he didn't comment. Bryony made no overtures to resume their friendship but thought of Rowan's words: 'She'll soon forget it, she needs you.' And he was right.

One morning Heidi came into the library where Bryony was studying the estate map.

'I just saw Justin go out,' the girl began. 'May I talk to you?'

Bryony waited.

'I'm sorry,' Heidi blurted out. 'I shouldn't have said what I did. I want us to be friends again. Please?'

Bryony looked at her anxious face.

'Well . . . ' she began teasingly, then put her arms round the younger girl. 'Of course. It's forgotten. Don't let's mention it again.'

*　*　*

'How would you like an outing this morning?' Justin asked some days later as she was about to settle at the computer.

'Outing?' she queried.

'I have to go to the church. The Rector has promised to look out the appropriate parish registers for Sir Andrew's birth, marriage and death. Would you like to come?'

She agreed at once and went to fetch a jacket. It could hardly be classed as a jolly outing, but to go would make her feel as if she was really participating in the research.

'The church is in the centre of the village, isn't it?' she asked as she climbed into his car. 'I've seen it from the outside.'

The car was large and sleek, very different from Rowan's workhorse estate car. She sank into the luxuriously soft upholstery, wishing they were going farther than the village.

'Justin! Good morning. How nice to see you.' The Rector came beaming down the path to meet them and escorted them into the church.

'I've brought Miss Redland, my secretary,' said Justin.

The Rector grasped Bryony's hand in his large one. 'How nice to meet you, Miss Redland. Is it your first visit to our lovely old church?'

She told him that it was and looked around with interest. The church had the cold, slightly musty smell of many old buildings, but the barrel-vaulted ceiling was beautiful and it had some surprisingly bright stained-glass windows.

'There's been a church on the site since nine hundred and ninety,' said the Rector. 'This building dates from the twelfth century. When you've finished with the registers, you must see our crusader. We're very proud of him.' He ushered them into the vestry. 'I've got the registers ready for you.'

For the next half hour, they pored over the old leather-bound books.

Bryony was fascinated to read the entry for the marriage between Andrew Henry Darke of this parish and Isabella Berowne of Axminster in the County of Devon. It was written in the thin, spidery hand of the nineteenth century.

'I believe her family weren't wealthy,' said Justin, 'so the marriage took place in the groom's house and not the bride's.'

Justin and the Rector began to talk together and, finding herself forgotten, Bryony wandered out of the vestry and went in search of the crusader the Rector had mentioned.

She found him, a worn stone figure with a battered nose, lying with his stone wife against the altar. She marvelled that they had been lying there for hundreds of years and wondered whether their faces as portrayed in stone were what they'd really looked like in life.

'Ah, you've found him,' said a voice behind her, and she turned to find the two men had left the vestry.

'Not many small country churches have a crusader,' said the Rector with pride.

'What was his name?' she asked.

'It's thought he was Sir Hugh de l'Auriac. The de l'Auriacs owned lands around here. But we're not sure. There's nothing to tell us definitely.'

At the door, he shook hands with them both and expressed the hope that he would see Bryony in church one Sunday.

'We'll find some coffee before we go home,' said Justin, guiding her across the square.

Bryony glanced towards the café. She would feel strange going in there with Justin. She almost wished they were going straight back to Greston Tower.

But rather than heading for the café,

he unlocked the car and soon they were heading out of the village.

She darted a quick glance at his profile. He was staring straight ahead, driving carefully to avoid the potholes in the narrow lane. He looked lost in thought and she had no wish to disturb him.

She was happy that their relationship had improved so much. She was no longer afraid of him, or afraid to speak her mind if she felt justified. And Justin himself seemed to have mellowed. He treated her almost as a colleague rather than an employee, and was plainly pleased with her enthusiasm for her job.

She sighed and looked out at the green and leafy countryside, just beginning to take on the red and gold autumn tints.

Justin glanced across at her.

'Does that sigh signify boredom or sadness?' he queried.

'Neither,' she assured him hastily. 'In fact, I was thinking how much I'm enjoying this work.'

He nodded. 'Good. And I'm enjoying your company and your assistance.' They smiled at each other in perfect harmony.

Ten minutes later, in the lounge of an old black and white hotel, Bryony settled herself in the corner of a huge leather settee. Justin sat in the opposite corner, and on a low table in front of them, a waiter placed a silver tray bearing a coffee pot and cups. There was cream and small chunks of brown sugar, and a dish of home-made shortbread.

Although the morning was warm, a log fire burned brightly on a huge stone hearth.

'This place is as old as the church,' Justin told her, looking around. 'Not in its present form, of course, but there's been a hostelry here since the twelfth century.'

'Are you going back as far as you can with the family history?' she asked.

'No. It's not really a family history. It's the story of Sir Andrew and

Greston Tower. Of course, we'll touch on earlier generations — probably in the introductory chapter.'

'Are you going to India to research the estates there?' she asked, smiling mischievously.

'Oh, you'd like a trip to India? I'm afraid that won't be necessary. There are plenty of notebooks, diaries and photographs, even press cuttings, to deal with that part of his life. And, of course, things are very different in India now.'

'I wonder why Sir Andrew decided to build Greston Tower here?' she mused.

'There has been a house on the site for hundreds of years, but he embellished and enlarged it. The house as you see it now is Sir Andrew's house. I suppose he wanted to 'make a statement', as they say. Many gentlemen of means in those days had the same idea.'

'I've enjoyed looking for differences between the old house and the new,' she admitted.

'I can tell.' He smiled at her. 'I'm not

sure Miss Gladstone would have enjoyed it so much. Now, if you've finished your coffee, I think we'd better go back.'

★ ★ ★

'I'll write up the notes on the church before lunch,' he said as they got out of the car. 'You can type them up this afternoon.'

'What shall I do just now?'

'I'm sure there's some post you can deal with — you only have an hour to fill before lunch. Thank you for your company.' He strode away into the house leaving her standing on the drive.

The house glowed with the golden sunlight of early autumn. She looked around at the soft countryside beyond the tower grounds — undulating green fields and low hills topped with clumps of trees like miniature forests, and knew, though it was quiet and remote, she would enjoy living here.

★ ★ ★

There were to be guests at dinner that night and as soon as her work was finished, Bryony went to her room to prepare. She wasn't conceited enough to want to stand out, but, on the other hand, she didn't want to be ignored. And after the 'schoolma'am' taunts of Carla Willard, she wanted to make a different impression.

She lifted her new pink dress from the wardrobe, shook out the long skirt and studied her reflection with satisfaction. Yes, a good choice.

The girls had spent a happy morning in Bardley a few days before, and although Bryony had hoped to see the theatre there had been no time. She had wanted to buy two dresses at least, and anything else that caught her eye, before they had to be back at Greston Tower at one.

'Nothing for me,' Heidi had told her cheerfully. 'This is a shopping trip just for you.'

She had parked the car and they had set off to try the shops in the main street. In the second, Bryony had found a stunning dress of deep, almost midnight blue.

'Beautiful,' Heidi had breathed when she emerged from the fitting-room and twirled for inspection. 'It really compliments your colouring.'

'It's kind of expensive,' Bryony had said, consulting the tag with a grimace, 'but blow it, I'm going to have it anyway! I still have my birthday money from Uncle Chris — I'll use that.' She had looked at her reflection again and nodded with satisfaction. 'This'll be perfect for looking really dressed up.'

At the town's only department store, she had found another dress, cerise pink this time.

'You don't think it's a bit bright?' she had asked Heidi anxiously.

'It's lovely,' the younger girl had assured her. 'No one will miss you in a crowd. But it's classy, too.'

They had arrived back with the two

dresses, a grey trouser suit and a hurriedly purchased assortment of tops and jumpers — and, on Bryony's part, a feeling that the morning had put them back on their old friendly footing.

Gazing now at her reflection, she decided that the colour was so vivid it needed the minimum of jewellery. Slim, silver pendant earrings and a silver bangle were enough.

Once she was ready to her satisfaction, she sat on the edge of the bed and waited for Heidi.

Headlights drew her to the window and she watched as two cars came up the drive and parked in front of the house. She glanced at the little gold clock on the dressing-table. If people were arriving, she had to go down. She couldn't wait any longer for Heidi.

The drawing-room was crowded, and as she stood in the doorway, feeling shy and awkward, she wished she had waited after all to come down with Heidi.

But then Justin spotted her and came over.

'You look lovely,' he said approvingly. 'What a gorgeous colour.'

He drew her into the room and made introductions.

'This is my new secretary, Miss Redland — Bryony,' he said. 'I'd like you to meet Colonel and Mrs Ralston, who are very old friends of mine. And Sylvia and Kenneth Stern — they run the cattery in the village.'

Bryony smiled shyly.

'Are you sure she's your secretary?' joked Colonel Ralston. 'She looks much too pretty and decorative for that.' He was a white-haired, oldish man with a whiskery moustache and twinkling eyes. He and his wife, a smiling, dumpy little woman, looked much older than Justin. Bryony liked them at once.

'We were friends of Justin's father,' explained Mrs Ralston. 'We've known Justin since he was a child.'

The other couple were nearer Justin's age. Sylvia Stern, tall, slim and elegant, looked faintly disapproving at the Colonel's joke. Kenneth Stern — who, Bryony discovered, was Sylvia's brother, not her husband — shook her hand and held it slightly too much longer than necessary. Feeling uncomfortable, she moved away from him as soon as she could.

Sylvia soon joined Carla and sat beside her to become immersed in a muttered conversation. They were obviously friends, thought Bryony, and hoped she wouldn't be another enemy.

'Where's Heidi?' asked Justin quietly at her elbow.

She turned to smile at him. 'She wasn't ready. I thought I'd better come down without her when I heard people arriving.'

He looked towards the door. 'I hope she won't be long.'

'We're waiting for two more guests,' he explained to the gathering at large. 'Guy Vernon, whom I think you all know, and his architect, Marcus Belling.' Even as he spoke, they heard Mrs

Buckley open the front door and greet some new arrivals.

Soon Guy Vernon appeared in the doorway, smiling and waving a hand. Behind him in the shadows stood a fair-haired man.

'I hope you don't mind,' Guy apologised, 'but Marcus couldn't come, so I've brought another friend, Kurt van Arne. Kurt's taking the publicity photographs of The Mill.'

Justin had stepped forward, a smile of welcome on his face, but now Bryony, watching him, saw the smile fade. Almost immediately, however, his good manners reasserted themselves and he shook hands with both men.

When he returned to Bryony's side, he was seething.

'This was deliberate,' he said. 'That man would do anything to get inside the house! But I can't blame Guy. He's been manipulated.' He looked round the room. 'Where on earth is that girl?' he muttered through clenched teeth.

'I'll go up to her room,' Bryony offered. 'Maybe she needs a hand with something — a zip, maybe . . .'

'No — wait. She's here. At least, I suppose it's her,' he said incredulously.

They looked at the figure who was posing in the doorway, her head held high. Heidi held the pose for a moment more, then wiggled — Bryony could think of no other way to describe it — her way the length of the room to take a drink from a tray.

'Sorry I'm late.' She smiled around the room. 'I couldn't fasten my dress.'

She caught sight of Kurt and for a moment the smile faded. She hadn't known he would be here, Bryony decided.

'I'm not surprised.' Carla gave a bitchy laugh. 'If you breathe out your zip will be in serious danger of bursting. How *will* you eat anything?'

Heidi ignored her and went over to the Ralstons. She was obviously a favourite with them.

'You little minx.' The Colonel

pinched her cheek. 'You've grown up much too fast.'

'What is she wearing?' Justin hissed each word separately at Bryony.

They both stared at the girl. Her dress was deep burnt orange, a sheath of satin as tight as it was possible to be. Her mouth was a gash of toning lipstick and huge pendant earrings swung to and fro as she moved.

'I — I'm sorry,' said Bryony, feeling she ought to apologise. 'I had no idea what she intended to wear.'

'It's not your fault,' he assured her. 'But she's gone too far. She'll be leaving for Scotland tomorrow. A few weeks with Aunt Morag will soon sort her out!'

Now was not the time to ask about Aunt Morag, Bryony decided, but she was obviously viewed as a punishment.

'Mr van Arne,' called Carla, 'do come and sit with us and tell us about your work. It must be so interesting. What sort of photographs are you taking of The Mill?'

Kurt looked surprised but gave a slight bow and took the seat next to her while Sylvia excused herself and went over to talk to Guy. Carla moved closer to Kurt, laughing extravagantly at his remarks, several times putting a hand on his arm. Trying to make Justin jealous, thought Bryony.

When Guy Vernon left Sylvia and wandered over to speak to Kurt, Carla grasped his hand and pulled him down to the seat on her other side, and Bryony watched with disgust as she flirted first with one man then the other. She had no doubt it was to annoy Justin, but he was more concerned with Heidi, who, obviously sensing his annoyance, stayed near Colonel and Mrs Ralston.

At dinner, Bryony found herself seated next to Kurt, who put himself out to be charming and attentive, and several times she felt Justin's eyes on her. It wasn't an altogether comfortable meal and she was glad when it was over.

They were taking coffee in the drawing-room when Guy called across to Justin, 'Would it be possible to see something of the house? I'd like to see more of the carved oak.'

Justin flashed a look of anger at Kurt but he was talking quietly to the Colonel and didn't look up.

Justin thinks this was Kurt's idea, thought Bryony. Of course, it's possible it was. Perhaps he suggested it to Guy before they arrived.

'Oh, Justin, that would be lovely,' Sylvia enthused. 'These old houses are so atmospheric.'

'And could we see your dear old Nanny Flake?' asked Mrs Ralston. 'I haven't seen her for months. Is she well?'

It was impossible for Justin to disappoint his guests. He crossed to the table where Bryony was pouring coffee.

'I'll have to agree,' he said in a quiet voice. 'Would you slip up to Nanny and ask if it's convenient?'

Of course, Nanny was thrilled. So many visitors at once. She put Pickle into the bedroom so that he wouldn't escape and told Bryony to assure Justin that she would love some company.

'I won't join you,' said Heidi, perching on the arm of the couch and picking up a magazine.

Justin looked meaningly at Kurt, daring him to stay behind, too. But Kurt was as eager as the others to see the house.

The tour began. The downstairs rooms were admired, but Justin's writing-room door remained unrevealed amongst the bookshelves. When they came to the little corridor leading to the music room, Justin caught Bryony's eye. Now what will he do, she wondered. He'd said it was his private room. Will he show everyone? But he led them firmly past the door and up the stairs.

They visited a little-used upstairs sitting-room and several empty bedrooms. Then they climbed twisting narrow stairs to the attic rooms.

Justin flung open a door with a

flourish. The old schoolroom, he announced.

'This is where I learned my letters and my father and grandfather before me.'

Bryony was fascinated. It was her first visit. Motes of dust danced in a shaft of light as the door was opened. A blackboard, still bearing some chalked letters, faced a long wooden table. In the corner was a battered rocking-horse with a straggly mane. Bookcases held an assortment of readers and children's story books.

'Where's the cane?' asked Guy with a laugh. 'There should be a long swishy one.'

'Were you a good little boy?' Sylvia teased.

'I believe so,' Justin said. 'There was a cane somewhere — ' he looked around vaguely ' — but I don't remember too many beatings. Our governess was a Miss Tait. She was strict but fair. I went away to school at eight so I don't remember much about those days. It seems a very long time ago.'

Bryony noticed that he said 'our governess'. Rowan had been a school-mate. She wondered whether the tragic Eleanor had been, too.

'We'll see whether Nanny is ready for us,' Justin said, shepherding them down the stairs. 'The other attic rooms were bedrooms for the maids years ago. They're not used now — except by spiders. I don't think you'd like to go in there.'

They knocked on Nanny's door and were received rapturously, but Bryony excused herself and went along the corridor to her own room. The dusty attic rooms had made her sneeze and she wanted a handkerchief.

In the bedroom, she opened a window and took deep breaths of the cool evening air. It was restful to be in the silent room after the chatter of the guests.

She found a clean handkerchief then left the room and set off down the corridor.

She decided not to rejoin the tour party. Nanny had enough people in her little apartment. She would go downstairs and talk to Heidi instead.

The door to the upstairs sitting-room had been left open. As she approached it, she was surprised to hear voices.

'You've been stringing me along.' It was Kurt's voice, angry. Obviously he had detached himself from the group. 'Why didn't you tell me Justin was dead against the modelling idea?'

A woman's voice answered quietly and it was impossible to make out the words.

'Well, his attitude was quite plain,' Kurt responded. 'I wouldn't have come if I'd known. And what are you going to get out of it if he agrees?'

At another murmur from the woman, Kurt gave a short laugh.

'Put you in the pictures? He'd love that, I'm sure! I suppose you want the publicity.'

Oh, Heidi, thought Bryony, you really love dicing with danger, don't you? If Justin comes down now and finds the two of you together . . .

She darted back to her bedroom, feeling dreadful about having overheard their conversation, but equally it would have been impossible to cross the open doorway without being seen. What a dilemma!

She opened her bedroom door silently and closed it again with a little bang this time. Then she walked slowly back towards the stairs.

She came upon Kurt standing in the doorway of the sitting-room, and behind him stood a guilty-looking Carla Willard.

So it wasn't Kurt and Heidi, but Kurt and Carla!

Downstairs, Carla had given the impression that she and Kurt were meeting for the first time. Yet quite clearly they were old acquaintances, if not friends. So Carla was conspiring with Kurt against Justin?

'Miss Redland,' Carla called out as Bryony drew level with them. 'I thought you were with the others.' She was obviously trying to assess whether Bryony had heard anything.

Bryony turned an expressionless face to her. 'I went to my room to fetch something.'

'We were just . . . ' Carla gesticulated towards Kurt, then, deciding that the secretary wasn't worth an explanation, stopped. 'Perhaps you would take Mr van Arne to join the rest.'

Kurt watched Carla descend the stairs with a strange expression on his face, before turning to Bryony.

'I'm sorry . . . ' he began.

'The others are with Nanny Flake,' she interrupted. 'I'll take you.'

Before they reached Nanny's door, it opened and the group came out, chattering. Justin was last. He turned from closing the door and, ignoring Kurt, looked levelly at Bryony.

She was annoyed to feel a flush stain her cheeks.

'Mr van Arne . . . ' she began, but Justin waved a hand and cut short her explanation.

'It really doesn't matter. Perhaps you both' — there was a slight emphasis on the last word — 'would like to join us in the drawing-room.'

For the rest of the evening, Justin ignored her, and Bryony quietly seethed. She had done nothing wrong even though he apparently suspected her of flirting with Kurt van Arne. Tomorrow she would confront him and expect an apology.

Two Proposals!

Bryony was woken next morning by a sound which puzzled her at first. Then realisation came. Rain! Heavy rain lashing against the window. The first since she'd arrived at Greston Tower. She had begun to think it was a place of eternal sunshine. She snuggled lower into the soft comfort of her bed.

Then she remembered last night and all feeling of comfort left her. Justin's expression as he came out of Nanny Flake's room and saw her with Kurt. The quiet fury on his face. The way he had ignored her for the rest of the evening. It was unfair because she had done nothing wrong.

There were voices in the corridor outside. The door opened and she looked up expecting to see Mrs Buckley with a tray of tea. But it wasn't Mrs Buckley. It was Heidi who entered, still in her dressing-gown and carrying a tray on which there were two cups and saucers.

'Good morning, Bryony. Except that it's *not* a good morning. And the rain's only part of it,' she grumbled.

She put a cup of tea on the bedside table for Bryony, and taking one for herself, perched on the end of the bed, tucking her feet under the duvet for warmth.

Bryony sat up and sipped her tea, giving the other girl a wan smile.

'I suppose you mean last night. Whatever possessed you to turn up dressed like that?'

'I wanted to look older.' Heidi's face was defiant. 'Older and self assured. I wanted Justin to think I could manage in London on my own.'

'It didn't work then. He was horrified. And Carla made it worse.'

'I hate her,' muttered Heidi. 'Her comments make Justin think I'm still a child.'

'And what about Kurt?'

'I honestly didn't know he was coming. I could have died when I saw him there.'

'I'm sure Justin thinks you had a hand in his appearance. He mentioned an Aunt Morag. Who's she?'

Heidi looked horrified. 'Oh no! Not Aunt Morag. He's threatened before but . . . D'you think he really meant it?'

'Meant what? Who *is* Aunt Morag?'

'She's my mother's aunt. Lance and I used to be sent to stay with her occasionally when we were younger. She lives in a gorgeous part of the Highlands but it's incredibly remote. You think this is quiet? You should try Lachlan Bridge!'

She swung her feet off the bed, crossed to the window and opened the drapes. The rain seemed to increase in strength and noise. Heidi stood gazing out.

'I wouldn't need fashionable clothes there,' she said bitterly. 'This is the weather, day after day after day. Boots and raincoats, that's all you need.'

'What about Aunt Morag?'

'Strict! Strict and straightlaced. I would be expected to help in the house and tell her where I was going every time I went out. Not that there's anywhere to go except for country walks. There's nothing to do and nobody to talk to. Justin couldn't be so cruel, could he?' She turned a stricken face to Bryony. 'You must help me. Persuade him not to send me there, please, Bryony.'

'You're not the only one out of favour with him,' Bryony pointed out.

'Who else? Not you, surely?'

'Afraid so.' She related the events of the evening, ending with, 'So he's as cross with me as he is with you.'

'But it was Carla's doing. Didn't you tell him?'

'There was no chance, but I'll tell him today, never fear. I won't be accused of something I haven't done.'

'Good for you! And promise you'll help me — somehow.'

'I'll do my best, that's all I can

promise. Let's see how this morning goes first. Now, I must dress — and so must you. Off you go and I'll see you at breakfast.'

★ ★ ★

When Bryony entered the library after breakfasting with Heidi, Justin was placing a pile of letters on her desk ready to be typed. His 'Good morning, Miss Redland,' was coolly polite.

She answered him in the same tone, sat at her desk and switched on her computer without looking at him.

Justin disappeared inside his writing-room, but a few minutes later he was out again and standing by her desk.

She continued to type and he crossed to the window and looked out at the rain.

'I think we'll have a fire in here today,' he said. 'It's not cold but it'll cheer the place up. What do you think?'

She stopped typing. Was this attempt

at friendly conversation a sign that he regretted his behaviour of last night? It was time to put the matter straight. She stood up.

'Mr Darke, last night I was asked to direct Mr van Arne back to the group. We hadn't been chatting together. In fact, I had no conversation with him except at the dinner table. You were wrong to draw conclusions otherwise without letting me explain.'

His eyes narrowed. 'You were asked? By whom?'

'By the person who *had* been talking to him. I came from my bedroom, walked past them, and was asked to return him to the group of guests.'

He nodded. 'I suppose you mean Heidi. She was afraid I would realise what she'd been up to if I saw her.'

'It wasn't Heidi.'

He frowned. 'Who else could it be? You must think I'm stupid if you think I'll fall for a story like that. No one else knows him well enough to leave my group of friends and go off to have a private conversation with him. Your loyalty to Heidi does you credit, but of course it was her,' he insisted.

Bryony hesitated. There was nothing for it.

She looked him straight in the eye. 'It was Miss Willard.'

His eyes flashed. 'Carla! But they only met last night. What would they have to say to each other in private?'

Bryony said nothing, and Justin turned back to the window.

After a few minutes, he said, 'I'm sorry I jumped to the wrong conclusion. I hope you weren't too upset. And of course I accept your word that it wasn't Heidi.' He said nothing about Carla.

Bryony returned to her typing and after turning as if to speak to her again then changing his mind, Justin left the room.

He hadn't returned by coffee time when, by working steadily, she had completed all the letters. She felt guilty about Carla. If only he had believed her about Heidi without demanding more information.

She stretched her arms above her head and waggled her head to and fro to ease the stiffness in her neck and shoulders. It had been a long typing session.

Why was she worrying about Carla Willard? That young lady was more than capable of defending herself! She would forget her and go and visit Nanny Flake instead.

She glanced out of the window at the rain-soaked garden, thinking again about Anila. How this weather must have depressed her.

But *she* wouldn't be depressed if she went to see Nanny Flake. She would cheer up any gloomy day.

She bumped into Heidi in the hall, wearing a raincoat and carrying a colourful umbrella.

'I'm keeping out of Justin's way!' she confessed. 'If he doesn't see me, perhaps he'll forget about Aunt Morag. You haven't spoken to him yet, I suppose?' She looked at Bryony hope-fully.

'Not yet, but I will.'

Heidi nodded and gave a quick glance towards the library door.

'I'll be back for dinner.'

'Dinner? But where are you going all day? The weather's awful.'

'I'll go into Bardley. I'll have lunch there and go to the cinema this afternoon. Alone,' she added meaning-fully. 'That should keep me away from Justin.'

As Heidi let herself out into the rain, Bryony ran up the stairs and along the corridor to Nanny Flake's apartment. As she raised her hand to tap on the door, she had a fleeting hope that Rowan would open it as before — but, of course, he wouldn't because he would be hard at work.

The door opened — and there stood Rowan. Bryony started to giggle.

'What? What is it?' he asked, looking perplexed.

'I wanted you to be here — and you

are. That's all,' she told him simply.

'Well, that's a lovely welcome. Come in. It's Bryony, Nanny,' he called over his shoulder.

Bryony was fussed over and soon the three of them were enjoying buttered scones with their coffee. Nanny was still excited about the visitors of the night before, and told Rowan all about them.

'My little room was crammed,' she said. 'They couldn't sit down. But it was so nice to see Mrs Ralston again. She's promised to call in one day for a cup of tea and a chat.'

Rowan stood up. 'Well, I'd better get back to work. Is there any chance you could be free for lunch today?' he asked Bryony.

She knew she should check with Justin, but she was feeling defiant. And she had to have lunch, after all.

'I'd love it,' she said.

'Right. Be at the steps at one and I'll sweep up and carry you off. Don't walk down the drive. If this rain keeps up, you'll be soaked.'

★　★　★

Justin was in the library when she went back downstairs.

'I've been for coffee with Nanny,' she said. 'By the way, I'm going out to lunch at one. Is that all right?'

She waited for queries but he said nothing except a brief, 'Of course. And don't hurry back.'

They spent the rest of the morning looking through boxes of old photographs. He wanted to choose some to illustrate the book.

'We'll include quite a few,' he said. 'I hate social history books with just a few illustrations in the middle. And we have so many here.'

Bryony was fascinated. Fading sepia prints of overdressed ladies and gentlemen in the garden; children with ringlets, big hats and button boots; elderly men with faces almost obscured by whiskers.

'It's possible to have damaged photographs restored,' he said, 'but I don't think we'll bother with those. We have plenty others to choose from.'

Bryony was sorting eagerly. 'I wonder if there's one of Anila?' she mused.

'No. Not one,' he told her firmly.

'But there are plenty of photographs from the time when she was living at the Tower. Why none of her?' she wondered.

He shrugged. 'Either they were destroyed or they're somewhere in the house and we haven't found them. I'll have the portrait photographed and include that.' He glanced at his watch. 'Ten to one. You'd better go and prepare for your lunch date.' He didn't look at her as he spoke.

He's guessed, she thought. He's guessed that I'm going out with Rowan. And if he's in here when Rowan comes for me, he'll see his car.

She tried to stroll nonchalantly from the room but had the uncomfortable feeling that she had disappointed him.

He's getting under my skin, she thought irritably. Does he want to control me the way he controls Heidi?

Heidi! She had forgotten her promise to tackle him about Aunt Morag. She would have to do it when she got back. There was no time now.

★   ★   ★

The rain had stopped when she emerged from the house and went down the steps. Rowan's car was waiting and pulled away as soon as she climbed in.

'Sorry if I'm late,' she said. 'We were busy.'

'Never mind, you're here now. How long can you be away?'

'Justin said not to hurry back, but I don't want to be more than an hour if it's possible.'

'We won't go far. Bar snack suit you?'

'Fine.' She settled back in her seat and relaxed. She hadn't decided whether to mention last night. A companionable silence settled between them.

Rowan turned into the car park of a small inn and they chatted about nothing in particular as they went inside and found a seat by the window.

'I'm going to have a ploughman's,' said Rowan, looking at the menu chalked on a blackboard. 'What about you?'

'I don't think so.' She laughed. 'Justin might not appreciate it if I breathe raw onion all over him this afternoon.'

Instead she chose turkey sandwiches made with delicious home-made bread.

'I envy him having you for a secretary,' Rowan observed. 'Wouldn't you like to come and work for me?'

'I studied history, not zoology,' she pointed out with a smile. 'I'd be no use to you.'

He gave a theatrical sigh and applied himself to his bread and cheese.

'We haven't met since the party. Did you enjoy it?' He was looking at her hopefully.

'Of course.' She thought of the dancing, not the crowds. 'Your friend

Andy was charming. And Fiona has invited me to a make-up party at her house next month.'

He gave her a wide smile. 'I hoped you'd make some friends.'

He toyed with his glass and looked into the fire.

'Do you think,' he began, still not looking at her, 'do you think you could live here permanently? Would you be happy? Or would it be too quiet for you?'

'Are you offering me a job? Do you really need a secretary?' She began to laugh, but stopped at the look on his face.

'I'm serious, Bryony. I am offering you a job — as my wife. Darling Bryony, will you marry me?'

She was stunned into silence. She looked at him, a bewildered expression on her face.

'But we hardly know each other!'

'I know all I need to know,' he said. 'I fell in love with you the day I met you, when I picked you up after you fell off the fence.'

She looked at him. This was going too fast.

'You like me, don't you?' he urged. 'We get on well together. In time, it could turn into love.'

'Is that a basis for marriage?'

He shrugged. 'Many people have married with less. Will you think about it? I'm rushing you, but I don't want to lose you. In a few months you'll be gone. Please say you'll think about it.' He took her hands in his, leaned forward and gently kissed her cheek. Then he cupped her chin in his hand and gently pressed his lips against hers.

Bryony felt nothing; not a spark, not a tingle. This was Rowan, whom she had secretly had such romantic dreams about. Rowan, in whose arms she had danced blissfully for an evening.

Confused, she pulled away from him, thankful the bar was almost empty.

'Rowan, I don't know what to say. I like you so much and, as you say, we get on well, but marriage . . . ' she shook her head.

'Just think about it,' he repeated. 'Now you know how I feel, there's no need to hurry.'

She looked at her watch. She had a desperate feeling that she wanted to get away, to think about this unexpected proposal.

'Yes, we'll go now,' he said. She had a feeling he was disappointed but was determined not to show it. 'I'll ring you in a few days. Not for a decision,' he added hastily, seeing her startled expression. 'Just for a chat. We'll fix a dinner date.'

They completed the short drive to Greston Tower in silence again, but this time it wasn't easy or companionable. Bryony looked out at the dripping countryside. The rain had stopped but everywhere was wet and gloomy. She longed to be back inside the Tower near the cheerful log fire in the library. It hadn't been a successful lunch and it was her fault. Surely, feeling about Rowan as she thought she did,

marriage would be the happiest out-
come?

★ ★ ★

Despite her protests, he turned in at the
gate, drove swiftly up the drive and
stopped at the foot of the steps. He
doesn't care who sees him now, she
thought in dismay.

She squeezed his hand and jumped
out of the car before he could kiss her
again.

As she climbed the steps, the front
door opened — and she was looking
into Justin's unsmiling eyes. Her stomach lurched, her heart flipped over
— and in a flash she realised why
Rowan's kisses, Rowan's proposal
meant nothing. She was in love, wholly
and completely in love, with Justin
Darke.

Colour flooded her cheeks. 'I'm not
late, am I?'

'Of course not. I told you not to
hurry back.' He closed the heavy door

and walked past her to the library. He showed no interest in her companion though he must have seen Rowan's car. 'When you're ready, we'll have a talk about your future.'

Her future? For a wild moment she envisaged another proposal. But the recollection of Justin's stern expression as he'd opened the door banished that idea as foolish.

When she followed him into the library, she found him seated in an armchair near the window, below the painting of Sir Andrew, and she was impressed again by the resemblance between the two men. Had Sir Andrew sat there to talk to Anila? She hoped his expression had been less severe if he had!

Justin indicated the chair opposite and she seated herself coolly, determined not to let him see her apprehension.

'Miss Redland, when you first came, I mentioned a probationary period, at the end of which you could decide whether you wanted to stay, and I could decide whether — ' he paused ' — whether we suited each other.'

I wonder why he's chosen today, after my lunch with Rowan, to bring this up, she thought.

'I have to tell you that I've heard from my secretary, Miss Gladstone, this morning. Her operation was a success, but she has decided not to return to Greston Tower and her position here. I believe she's moving to the seaside to live with a cousin.' He waved a hand in dismissal of Miss Gladstone.

'So you're saying that you now need a permanent secretary?' Bryony ventured. Was he also saying that she would not be suitable?

He nodded. 'Someone who won't mind working under pressure. The book on Sir Andrew is an indulgence. When that's finished, I must go back to my real work. Perhaps that wouldn't be so interesting for you.'

What could she say? Should she beg him to keep her? Should she say she would do anything to be near him? No, she must be businesslike; point out that she had all the necessary qualifications to be his permanent secretary.

It was too late. He looked at her sharply.

'Perhaps the position doesn't appeal to you on a permanent basis.' He stood up. 'Think about it and let me know this evening. If you want it, we'll have another talk.

'I've left a list of books on your desk. Could you collect them from the shelves, please? And do take care on the ladder.'

He disappeared into his room and Bryony was left staring into space. There had been a coolness in his voice. Would he prefer her to leave? Did he want the chance to interview other girls and choose a new secretary?

Or was the coolness the result of seeing her get out of Rowan's car? She had defied him and gone out of her way to be friendly with Rowan. Why should he want to keep her? But how could she bear to leave?

She crossed to the desk and picked up the list of books, then moved the ladder to the appropriate area. There were two books on very high shelves and one halfway up. Climbing carefully to the top of the ladder, she selected the first two books and tucked them under her arm.

She descended and stopped near the third book. She had to stretch to the left to reach it. She knew she should climb down and move the ladder. But she stretched a little further . . .

With a crash, the two books under her arm fell to the floor.

Justin's door flew open and he rushed out.

'Bryony! What happened? Are you all right?' He reached up, put his hands round her waist, and lifted her down. 'I thought you'd fallen!'

He held her, and then, as if suddenly aware of what he was doing, he dropped his hands.

Bryony stooped and retrieved the books. 'I'm so sorry, I hope they're not damaged. I should have got down and moved the ladder.' She was babbling to cover her confusion. He had called her 'Bryony'. He had rushed out as if he was concerned about her. She could still feel the pressure of his hands on her waist. Did he — could he, care about her?

A prosaic voice in her head told her that he was probably worried about the books, but she ignored it.

Justin was smiling ruefully and shaking his head.

'I told you to take care on the ladders.'

'I'm sorry to have disturbed you,' she said. 'I'll be all right now. I'll collect the rest of the books.'

'No. Leave them for a while. We'll have a cup of tea.'

He waved her to the armchair again and picked up the telephone to ask Mrs Buckley to bring tea.

Remembering her promise to Heidi, Bryony decided this might be a good time to plead for the younger girl.

'Mr Darke, could we talk about Heidi?' she asked.

'I rather thought we might talk about you,' he returned.

'I promised Heidi I would speak to you,' she persisted.

'Very well. I suppose it's the Kurt van Arne thing.'

'She's very sorry about last night. She was trying to show you that she's grown up and able to manage in London on her own.'

'Funny way of showing it!' he growled.

'She would really hate to be sent away with her Aunt Morag.'

'I'm sure he would,' he returned dryly.

'So — I've an alternative idea,' she went on, ignoring his interruption. 'Could she go and stay with my Aunt Margaret for a few weeks? Cardiff isn't remote like the Scottish Highlands. She'd have shops and entertainment but she'd still be away from — well, you know.'

'You've mentioned this to your aunt?'

'No, not yet. I thought I'd better speak to you first. But I know she'll agree. She loves young people and Heidi will be company for her. She says she misses me.'

He smiled. 'I'm sure she does.' He gazed thoughtfully out of the window. 'So — you've decided you want to stay?' He turned back to her. 'If you're making plans for Heidi, you must have decided to stay.'

'Is it up to me?' she asked quietly.

'Well, *I* want you to stay,' he replied. 'You're hard-working, you're easy to get on with, and — ' he smiled ' — you're very decorative! A desirable attribute in a secretary.'

She coloured up and put her hand against the cheek nearest to him to conceal it.

He smiled. 'I love the way you blush. So few girls nowadays have the delicacy to respond to a compliment in that way. But I'm sorry, I didn't mean to embarrass you.'

'What about Heidi?' she persisted.

'If your aunt is agreeable, then so am I. Phone her tonight and I'll speak to Heidi about it tomorrow. Would you like some more tea?'

She shook her head. 'No, thanks. I'd better get on with finding those books or I'll have done nothing this afternoon. What shall I do after that?'

Before he could answer, the door opened noisily and Carla Willard strode into the room, drawing off her gloves. She made for the fire and stood warming her back as she surveyed them.

'How very cosy,' she drawled. 'Tea for two.'

Justin stood up. 'Would you like a cup, Carla? We can send for a fresh pot.'

'We can have some while we're out,' she replied, smiling sweetly. 'Have you forgotten you promised to take me to Craig's exhibition?'

His brow furrowed. 'Craig's — ? I'm afraid I *had* forgotten. But I don't know whether artistic metalwork is quite my thing.'

'Craig will be very hurt if we don't go,' Carla coaxed. 'After all, we promised.'

'Very well.' He turned back to Bryony. 'I'm sorry about this. Perhaps you'd like to do a bit of research while I'm out. See what you can discover about the tea clippers. Make some notes and we'll look at them when I get back.'

'Bye-ee.' Carla fluttered her fingers triumphantly at Bryony as they left the room. 'Don't work too hard!'

An Enchanted Evening

Bryony remained immobile, looking at the door for five minutes after they left. How could she fight Carla Willard? Even when Justin had reason to be annoyed with her, he seemed willing to do as she asked. And Carla was so smug about it.

Slowly she got to her feet. Better get on with collecting the books — and carefully this time.

The job accomplished, she looked at her watch. Four o'clock. Would Aunt Margaret be in?

She was, and delighted to hear from her niece. After the usual greetings and inquiries about the family, Bryony broached the subject of her call.

'How would you like some company for two weeks?'

'Bryony! You've got some time off. How lovely.'

'No, not me,' Bryony put in hastily. Briefly she outlined the problem. 'Heidi just isn't the sort of girl to be buried in the Scottish Highlands,' she said. 'But she needs to get away from the situation here. Frankly, I don't think she can handle it. And Justin is so cross with her.'

'Send her to us,' said Aunt Margaret briskly. 'We'll look after her. We'll show her around, give her something different to think about. It's a pity Simon's away, he could have taken her out.'

'Bless you,' said Bryony. 'She'll be so grateful. I'll phone later with the details.'

However, grateful wasn't exactly Heidi's reaction when told of the plan.

'Cardiff! I don't want to exchange Scottish mountains for Welsh ones!'

'Cardiff isn't in the mountains.' Bryony was stung by the other girl's reaction. 'It's a beautiful city with a lovely civic centre, plenty of shops and a castle on the riverbank.'

'Mm.' Heidi was thoughtful. 'Plenty of shops.'

'All sorts. And clubs and restaurants and parks and cinemas.'

'Mm,' she said again. 'And your aunt doesn't mind?'

'On the contrary, she's looking forward to having you. You'll love her — and Uncle Chris.'

'What about your cousin — Simon, isn't it?'

'Oh, he's away on a training scheme somewhere. But Aunt Margaret will show you around.'

'And Justin?'

'He agreed — eventually.'

Suddenly Heidi flung her arms around Bryony's neck.

'Thank you. I knew you'd think of something. When can I go?'

'Justin will speak to you about it this evening.'

'D'you know, I'm looking forward to it. It will be an adventure after all. Cardiff is in another country, isn't it?'

Bryony laughed at the happy face

before her. What a mercurial creature she was, always up or down.

'Shall I understand everyone? They won't expect me to speak Welsh, will they? How do I say 'Hello'?'

' 'Bore da' will do. But I can assure you they all speak English!'

It was arranged that Bryony should drive Heidi down to Cardiff the next morning, stay the night and return the following day.

'You won't need your car there,' Justin told Heidi, 'so if Bryony takes you it'll be an opportunity for her to see her family.'

As the girls headed for Wales, Bryony had a twinge of regret that she was leaving the field open for Carla, but, as she told herself bitterly, there was really no contest. Carla was already in possession. Justin would never think of her, Bryony, as anything more than a secretary.

'How long will it take to get there?' asked Heidi.

'Two to three hours. It isn't very far.

We'll easily be there by lunchtime.'

It was midweek. The motorway wasn't very busy and they made good time. By a quarter to twelve they were driving past the gleaming white buildings of the civic centre.

'There's the castle,' Heidi pointed. 'Look at the stone animals peeping over the wall. And I can see the towers. Where does your Aunt Margaret live?'

'She doesn't live in Cardiff itself but in a little town five miles away. It's called Penarth. It's a seaside resort.'

Heidi went quiet. Bryony glanced at her. 'What's the matter?'

'It isn't remote, is it?'

'Remote!' Bryony was exasperated. 'It's five miles from the city, with plenty of trains and buses. And Aunt Margaret has her own car. You won't be stranded, I can assure you. Here we are . . . '

They turned into the drive of a large detached house and soon Bryony was clasped in the embrace of a plump, motherly woman.

'Aunt Margaret! How lovely to see

you. This is Heidi.'

There were greetings inside when Uncle Chris came in from the garden and soon they were all sitting round the table and tucking into a generous lunch. Bryony looked happily at her uncle and aunt. They would give Heidi a good time; perhaps even make her eat more than she usually did.

'Let's go for a walk this afternoon,' she suggested. 'We've been sitting a long time.'

Uncle Chris excused himself. He had things to do in the garden, he said.

'He's not keen on walks,' Aunt Margaret confided to Heidi. 'Thinks they're pointless. But we'll go.'

A fifteen-minute stroll from the house brought them out on to a grassy cliff walk. The sea was slate grey, but the air was fresh and invigorating. They strolled along the cliff top, down a steep hill and on to the promenade.

'Look! A pier,' Heidi exclaimed. 'And palm trees.'

'It's an Edwardian town,' said Aunt

Margaret. 'They loved piers and palm trees. Let's have a cup of tea in the café at the end before we go back.'

'I think I'm going to enjoy it here.' Heidi's cheeks were flushed from the wind. 'It's like being on holiday.'

'I hope it *will* be a holiday for you, my dear,' said Bryony's aunt.

After tea, Heidi excused herself and said she would like an early night. Excitement had made her tired.

'I expect she's being tactful,' said Bryony. 'Giving us the chance to talk. She's a sweet kid really.'

She sat by the fire with her aunt and uncle and told them about her job, and about the feud between Justin and Rowan.

'It's just like one of his books,' said her aunt. 'What's he like, Mr Sancerre? Is he handsome? I imagine him tall and romantic looking. I've never seen a picture of him.'

'He doesn't like photographs on the dust jackets of his books,' said Bryony. 'He's a very private sort of person.

That's why he's so cross with Kurt van Arne and his scheme to feature Justin and Greston Tower in a magazine.'

'Quite right, too,' said Uncle Chris. 'A man has a right to privacy, however famous he is.'

'But is he handsome?' persisted Aunt Margaret.

Bryony pictured his face so close to hers as he lifted her from the ladder.

'Yes, he is handsome. Very handsome.'

Uncle Chris gave her a quizzical look.

'You haven't fallen for him, have you? You'll only be there a few months. Don't get carried away.'

'Actually it may be more than a few months. It may be permanent.' She explained about Miss Gladstone. 'I'll let you know when I've absolutely decided.'

She had decided and so had Justin, but she wanted to hug the knowledge to herself for a while longer.

'Are you happy there? Is it what you expected?'

'Look at her.' Her uncle laughed. 'Doesn't she look happy?'

'It's a wonderful job and I'm very happy,' smiled Bryony, kissing them both goodnight. 'Thank you for having Heidi. We're all very grateful to you.'

★ ★ ★

She was up early the next day, breakfasted and away before Heidi was awake. She would phone her later. Her heart sang as she covered the miles back to Greston Tower — and the man she loved.

Justin himself opened the door to her. He must have been watching from the library window, she thought. He drew her inside with an eagerness which was echoed in his welcoming smile.

'Bryony! You're back.' He took her overnight case and placed it on the bottom stair. Then he ushered her into the library, calling to Mrs Buckley for coffee.

'Is Heidi settled?' he asked her.

'Very much so. She and my aunt have made plans for days ahead. I don't think she'll be rushing back.'

'It's very kind of your aunt. And of you. When I asked you to help with Heidi, I couldn't have imagined how successfully you would do it.'

Bryony drank her coffee standing in front of the log fire.

'It's lovely to be back.'

'You've just left your home and you can say that,' he said in wonder.

She couldn't meet his eyes. This is my home. Home is where you are, she thought. But that could never be said aloud. He was her employer and his delight at her speedy return was undoubtedly connected with work and how soon they could return to it. She looked towards her desk.

'Have you lots for me to type?' she asked with a smile.

'I read around a very interesting topic last night,' he said. 'Bella Berowne.'

'Sir Andrew's wife? The actress?'

'Yes. We have a large box of theatre programmes and press cuttings. She was a big fish in a small pond, of course, but very popular. I'll show you the notes and the photographs.' He disappeared into his room.

Bryony looked around. How dear this house — this room — had become in a short time.

Justin came back with a pile of photographs which he spread out on the large table. They were in soft sepia tints, some oval in shape. Bryony joined him and picked up several in turn.

Bella Berowne was a smiling lady with the buxom figure of the time. She wasn't conventionally pretty but had huge liquid brown eyes and thick hair, padded out on either side of her face.

Most of the pictures showed her in stage costume; swirling skirts, dresses lavishly covered with lace, and huge, beribboned hats.

'She was a singer first of all,' explained Justin. 'She appeared in most of the musicals of the day. But she also acted in straight plays. Here she is in 'Lady Windermere's Fan'.'

Bryony studied the glamorous photograph.

'However will you choose? They're all fascinating.'

'That's where you come in. I want you to make a short-list of ten, then I'll make the final choice.'

Bryony smiled delightedly. This was just the sort of task she enjoyed.

Justin walked towards the door, then turned back.

'By the way, we're dining early this evening. I have tickets for the theatre at Bardley. I thought you might like to see the scene of Great-grandmama's triumphs.'

She picked up another photograph, her hands unsteady. She was going to the theatre with Justin! They would drive there, and drive back, just the two of them.

Her heart was racing and she had to force herself to settle to the job in hand.

Of course, it was just for research, but she could dream, couldn't she?

* * *

That evening she dressed carefully in a long black skirt and black velvet bolero. A frothy white blouse took away the severity of the outfit. She felt quite Edwardian. Justin looked at her with approval when she joined him in the hall. He said nothing, but his smile was comment enough.

The journey to Bardley took only fifteen minutes. Justin parked and they were soon in the circle bar.

'Of course, it may be absolutely awful,' he murmured, 'but amateurs are so much more professional nowadays so we'll hope for the best.'

Bryony studied her programme. ' 'The Merry Widow'. I've seen this before. It has some lovely songs in it.'

'We're lucky they're doing something in which she appeared,' he said. 'It'll give us a better idea of how she would look on the stage.'

'What a good thing they're not doing 'Guys And Dolls'!' she commented with a grin.

The bell rang and they made their way to their seats. She looked around the auditorium with interest.

'It has been redecorated since her day and there may be some structural differences,' Justin said, 'but it's a listed building so it won't have changed very much.'

The auditorium wasn't large but retained its Edwardian elegance. It had two stage boxes and above the red plush seats hung a huge, sparkling chandelier.

The seats were filling up and there was an expectant buzz amongst the audience.

'Mostly relations of the cast, I expect,' said Justin, 'so they'll be especially appreciative.'

A few minutes later Bryony had to stand up, hugging her coat and bag, so that another couple could pass to their own seats. As she prepared to sit again, she looked down into the stalls and saw, chattering animatedly in the centre row below her, Rowan and a blonde girl. The girl had upswept hair and was wearing something elegant in black. Gold earrings and a gold necklace flashed as they caught the light.

Bryony thought of his proposal to her. It hadn't taken him long to find consolation!

Justin followed the direction of her gaze and smiled at her.

'Yes, Rowan's here. Of course you must speak to him if you want to. Don't mind me.'

'He seems to be occupied,' said Bryony, trying to keep her voice light.

'Ah, the beautiful Stella,' said Justin, and his tone wasn't altogether complimentary.

'You know her?'

'Everyone knows her. Sometime television actress. That's her husband next to her.'

'Oh.' Bryony hadn't noticed the small, plump man next to the girl. She looked questioningly at Justin.

'He's loaded,' he told her. 'Local manufacturer. Able to give her whatever she desires.'

She sat back in her seat. Justin was revealing an ironic side she hadn't seen before. She supposed it was the side that enabled him to write successful novels. So far she had only seen his serious side.

The conductor entered and the overture began. The curtains opened and, abandoning her thoughts, Bryony settled down to enjoy the show.

In the interval, she sipped a glass of wine thoughtfully.

'Did Bella play the Widow?' she asked.

'There are a few photographs which suggest her in that part. They're unlabelled, unfortunately. But she seems to have played all the leads so it's probable. You must take a look through the old programmes and see if I've missed one for 'The Merry Widow'.'

Surreptitiously Bryony's eyes flickered round the bar, searching for Rowan. But it was so crowded, it was impossible to see everyone.

The bell rang for the second act and they returned to the auditorium. She glanced down to the stalls. The trio were already in their seats. Perhaps they hadn't bothered with a drink.

Justin must have read her thoughts.

'Some people go to the hotel opposite in the interval,' he observed. 'Less crowded.'

She didn't know whether to be pleased or disappointed that she and Rowan hadn't met.

She glanced at Justin. He was scribbling furiously in a notebook.

'Atmosphere,' he whispered. She nodded.

The orchestra struck up, the curtains swept open and the smell of paint and size and make-up was wafted into the auditorium. Bryony gazed at the stage, entranced.

The ballroom costumes were lavish,

reflecting the photographs of Bella Berowne. As the leading lady weaved in and out, partnered by elegant men in evening dress or impressive uniforms, Bryony imagined Bella in the role of Hanna Glavari, the Merry Widow. The leading lady sang beautifully; danced seductively, fluttered her fan and flirted with all the men. So would Bella Berowne have, Bryony was sure. This was exactly what a night at the theatre at the beginning of the nineteen hundreds would have been like.

She flashed a glance at Justin. His concentration was completely on the colourful scene before them. What was he thinking? She was conscious of his arm as it pressed against hers. She longed to take his hand and feel the warm pressure of his fingers. What would he do if she did?

Embarrassed by her thoughts, she moved slightly away from him. If he noticed, there was no sign. He continued to study the stage.

They clapped vigorously when it ended, exchanging smiles of enjoyment.

'Just what we needed to put us in the mood for Bella Berowne,' Justin commented. 'Come on, this way.'

They followed the crowds of people as they made their way, humming the tunes softly, down the stairs and into the foyer.

Rowan stood alone against the far wall. She was struck by how like Justin he looked in a dark suit instead of his casual everyday clothes.

'I'll see you outside in five minutes,' Justin murmured, moving away.

'Why does he assume I need to speak to Rowan?' she thought. But all the same she made her way across the foyer towards him.

A smile lit up his face. 'Bryony! I didn't know you were here. Are you on your own?'

So he hadn't noticed his cousin.

'I came with Justin.'

'With Justin? Gracious me!'

'Why not?' She was annoyed at his

response. 'We're doing research on Bella Berowne.'

'Of course. I'm sorry.' He had seen the irritation in her face. 'Bryony, have you thought about . . . '

'Here are your companions.' Bryony had noticed Stella approaching. 'I must go. I'll see you, Rowan.' She moved towards the door giving the blonde girl a slight smile as they passed.

Justin was waiting outside. 'Are you tired? Do you want to go straight back?' he asked.

'No, I'm not tired. Why?'

He gave her an enigmatic smile, and led the way to the car.

'Supper,' he said, as he started the engine. 'I know just the place.'

Twenty minutes later they were driving between an avenue of tall, thin trees towards a French-style manor house.

'It doesn't look like a hotel but it is,' he said. 'One of the best I know.'

The French theme was continued inside with white and gold furniture, heavily embossed floral wallpaper and huge bowls of flowers.

They were met by a very tall, exquisitely-dressed lady, who greeted Justin like a favoured friend. She conducted them to a small dining-room where tables were grouped round a log fire.

Justin helped Bryony with her coat and they were soon seated and studying the menu. Bryony's French was reasonably good, but she was beaten by the flowery writing and descriptions on the parchment menu.

'Would you order for me?' she asked, and immediately wondered whether he would be flattered or think her hopelessly ignorant.

His choice suited her perfectly. They had a seafood cocktail in a piquant lemony sauce and then small lamb noisettes with mint butter.

'That was delicious,' she said as she replaced her knife and fork.

'You've enjoyed this evening?'

She gave him a radiant smile. 'It's

been one of the most perfect I've ever had.' Then she felt herself colouring as he studied her closely.

'That little blush.' His voice was soft as he touched her cheek with his fingertips.

Shyly she looked down at the tablecloth.

'I mean it was a wonderful way of doing research.'

'Then perhaps we can do some more research another evening.'

She couldn't trust herself to look at him.

They walked to the car in silence. He held her arm, 'so that you won't trip,' he explained. She was almost delirious with happiness. If only this evening would never end.

* * *

The telephone was ringing as they entered the hall at Greston Tower. Justin went into the library to answer it, but called to Bryony as she was about to climb the stairs. 'It's Heidi for you. Do you want to take it in here?'

Bryony sat down at her desk and took the receiver from him.

'Hi, Heidi! How's it going?'

'Oh, Bryony.' Heidi's voice was breathless and excited. 'We've had a most wonderful evening. I had to tell you.'

'You and Aunt Margaret?'

'No. Me and Simon.' Heidi laughed happily. 'Bryony, he doesn't belong to you, does he? I mean, you're not interested in him, are you?'

'In Simon? Goodness, no! He's like a brother. Why?'

'Well — I think I could be *very* interested. You didn't tell me he was gorgeous.'

'Is he?' Bryony asked stupidly.

'Of course he is! And I think he's interested in me. We've been out all evening. He had tickets for a wonderful dance and then we walked along the cliff top and looked at the little lights on the boats in the channel.'

'But it's dark on the cliff walk at night,' Bryony pointed out.

'Simon had a big torch and we wrapped ourselves in his car rug and laughed so much. Oh, I've had such fun!'

Bryony thought she had never heard the younger girl sound so happy.

'I thought Simon was away,' she commented.

'He phoned home and Aunt Margaret told him about me and he came back.'

Bryony smiled to herself. Trust Simon! But she felt happy. Simon was infinitely better for Heidi than Kurt van Arne. Justin should be pleased, too.

'What have you been doing?' asked Heidi.

'Justin and I have been to the theatre at Bardley.' She tried to sound casual.

'A-ha,' said Heidi.

'What do you mean, 'A-ha'?'

'Oh, nothing. Did you have a nice time?'

'The most wonderful time. Of

course, it was research,' she added.

'Of course,' Heidi agreed solemnly.

'By the way,' Bryony went on, 'did Justin tell you that Miss Gladstone isn't coming back?'

'No!' There was an excited squeal from the other end. 'So it's goodbye dragon? How wonderful! Now you can stay on permanently.'

'Well, I haven't quite decided,' Bryony teased.

'You are! I've decided for you. I'll phone Justin and tell him so.'

'No, it's OK,' said Bryony hastily. 'It's all settled. I am staying.'

'Thank goodness. What a wonderful evening.' The other girl sighed. 'I shan't sleep for excitement. Well, goodnight, Bryony.'

Bryony replaced the receiver, murmuring to herself, 'I don't think I shall sleep for excitement either.'

And Justin had hinted that there could be more such evenings. What a pity Carla Willard was on the scene.

She looked at her reflection in the

bathroom mirror as she prepared for bed. Carla Willard. Wasn't she a match for Carla Willard?

She snuggled under the duvet prepared to go over each moment of the evening again. But in two minutes, she had fallen asleep.

Christmas

A week later, Justin sent her into Bardley to collect a list of books he had ordered from the library.

'I haven't really time to go myself, and anyway, it'll get you out of the house for a change,' he said. 'Don't hurry back, stay for some lunch.' He pressed some money into her hand, but when she pulled her hand back in protest, he shook his head. 'Don't be silly. It's expenses.'

In the town, she parked near the library and collected the books, taking them back to the car so that she wouldn't have to carry them around with her.

It was the first time she had visited Bardley on her own, but she could remember the layout. Most of the shops were in the main street behind the library, so she made her way there.

Christmas was only weeks away and the problem of Christmas presents loomed large. Her aunt and uncle were no problem — perfume for her, cigars for him. But what could she give the people at Greston Tower? And particularly, what on earth could she buy for Justin? The problem had already cost her many hours of thought.

The shops were already gaily decorated with many gift ideas in their windows. Almost at once she saw just the thing for Nanny Flake. A mannequin in the window of the department store was draped in a wide mohair stole in brilliant scarlet.

She went into the shop. Carols jingled over the sound system. As it was her first Christmas visit, they didn't annoy her. She made her way to the gift department, hoping to be inspired by its display. What could she give Heidi? Not clothes, not jewellery. Make-up? That was a possibility.

Then she saw it, the perfect gift for a budding model: a magnifying mirror which lifted up from its case, swivelled, angled, and when a switch was pressed, burst into light. Heidi would love it. The price made her pause for just a second, but she had to have it.

Next to the department store was a large bookshop. Simon was very keen on aviation. After a discussion with the owner of the shop, she left carrying the latest book on the history of flight.

Well satisfied with her purchases, she glanced at the clock on the Town Hall. It was past coffee time, but she could have an early lunch instead. She didn't want to be too late back in any case.

She spotted an Italian restaurant across the street. She loved Italian food, and it had the advantage of leaving you hungry after a few hours, so she wouldn't disappoint Mrs Buckley at dinner.

She ordered spaghetti carbonara, then looked around the restaurant with interest. In the corner was an old wooden handcart covered with imitation grapes and oranges. On the shelves above heavy-framed mirrors were the inevitable Chianti bottles. There were quite a few customers. Wouldn't it be nice if I knew someone, she thought. It would be pleasant to chat over a meal, rather than eat alone.

Even as she thought the thought, a voice spoke at her shoulder.

'Bryony. May I join you?'

She hadn't noticed him come in.

'Rowan!'

He was seated opposite her before she could say anything else.

'What a wonderful surprise!' he said, looking delighted. 'Are you waiting for anyone, Heidi or . . . '

'No, I'm on my own. Heidi's away for a week or two. I've just been to the library.'

'And shopping.' He glanced at her parcels.

'Christmas presents,' she explained. 'I'm quite pleased with my purchases this morning.'

Rowan studied the menu. 'Have you ordered?'

'Yes. Spaghetti carbonara.'

'All that cream!' He tutted, then grinned wickedly. 'I don't blame you. I'll have the same.'

They looked at each other. Please don't let him mention the proposal, she thought.

'Bryony, have you thought any more about — you know. What we discussed the other evening.'

Bryony twisted her fingers together. It was most embarrassing. She was very fond of Rowan. She didn't want to hurt him.

'Rowan, I'm very fond of you. You've been so kind to me from the beginning. But marriage is such a big step. I don't think I'm ready yet.'

'I could offer you a very comfortable life,' he coaxed. 'I have a nice house and you could work or not as you pleased. Of course, not with . . .'

'Not with Justin,' she finished for him. 'No, that would be very awkward.'

'I do love you, Bryony,' he pressed. 'And you say you're fond of me. I'd settle for that. Couldn't we take a chance?'

She was silent, looking away from him.

'Or — is there someone else?' he probed.

For her there was, but her feelings for Justin could never be returned so she answered quite honestly, 'No-one else is interested in me.'

The answer seemed to satisfy him.

'That means I have a chance. I'll ask you again after Christmas.'

She laughed. 'All right, after Christmas.'

The subject was forgotten and they settled to enjoy their lunch.

★ ★ ★

At the end of the following week, Simon brought Heidi back to Greston Tower, a changed Heidi, softer, less aggressive.

'Simon and I have been talking about my future,' she told Justin and Bryony.

195

Her guardian looked at her warily.

'You want me to go to college, don't you?' Heidi went on.

'Well?'

'Simon has had a brilliant idea.'

Justin looked at Simon and raised his eyebrows.

'There's a very good college in Cardiff where Heidi could study the things she's most interested in,' Simon explained.

'Yes. Fashion and design and make-up and all sorts of interesting things,' Heidi joined in. 'I could live with Aunt Margaret while I studied.'

Justin looked at Bryony. 'What do you think?'

'It's worth considering,' she conceded.

He nodded. 'We'll think about it then — after Christmas.'

Something else for after Christmas, thought Bryony as the young couple went off hand in hand.

'Do you have to go home for Christmas, Bryony?' asked Justin. 'Would your aunt and uncle mind very much if you stayed here instead?'

She looked at him, startled. 'Stay here? At Greston Tower? I — I don't know.'

'I'd love you to spend Christmas with us. And I know it would please Heidi.'

'I'll have to speak to my aunt. I'm sure she'll expect me home, but whether she'd mind if I stayed here, I don't know.'

'Ask her, please.'

She was surprised by the intensity of his gaze.

She phoned her aunt that evening.

'What a strange thing you should ask that,' her aunt told her. 'We had a letter this morning from Gisela — you remember, my friend in Austria. She wants Uncle Chris and I to spend the holiday with her.'

'Christmas in Austria? That would be so lovely!' said Bryony. 'Snow and sleigh rides, a real picture-book Christmas.'

'I had intended to write to her today

and explain that you and Simon would be coming home.' She paused. 'I wonder whether Simon . . . '

'Leave it to me,' said Bryony. 'Write to Gisela accepting. I have an idea about Simon.'

★ ★ ★

'My aunt and uncle have received an invitation to spend Christmas in Austria,' she told Justin. 'The problem was Simon and me. But if I stay here and Simon . . . '

'Simon must stay, too,' he said at once. 'Heidi will insist. We'll have a good old-fashioned Christmas.'

Bryony gave him a wicked glance. 'Do you intend to dress up as Father Christmas?'

'I don't think I'll go quite that far,' he said with a mock frown.

Mrs Buckley came in with a tea tray, closely followed by Heidi and Simon. Bryony gave Simon Justin's Christmas invitation.

'Mum's happy about it?' he asked.

'She'd like to go to Austria for Christmas so yes, she's happy about it.'

'Then I accept, and thank you very much, Justin.' He gave Heidi's hand a squeeze.

'It's a wonderful idea.' Heidi's face was shining. 'This will be such a perfect Christmas!' She was so happy, she almost forgot her figure and ate a whole cake, which amused Bryony greatly. Kurt van Arne was past history, she thought.

'By the way, what's happened to Carla?' asked Heidi. 'We haven't seen her for a while. Is she ill?'

'On the contrary.' Justin selected a sandwich. 'She's spending two weeks at a craft instruction course. Seems to be enjoying it very much.'

Heidi looked astonished. 'A course! I thought she knew all about crafts. What can they teach her?'

'She's doing the teaching. She's one of the instructors,' he told her.

He looked quite unconcerned by her

absence, Bryony thought. But it was only two weeks. Carla would be back to spoil Christmas, she was sure.

★ ★ ★

Two days before Christmas, Simon returned, accompanied by Lance, Heidi's brother. Bryony had met him a few times before and liked him very much. He was as dark as Heidi was fair and had an impish face and spiky hair.

When Simon went off somewhere with Heidi, Lance asked Bryony if she would like to go out with him.

'I still have a few presents to buy,' she told him. 'I thought I'd go shopping this afternoon.'

Lance made a rueful face. 'Shopping isn't quite what I had in mind.'

'It won't take long and I wasn't planning to go into town. There's a huge garden centre not far away with lovely ideas for presents. I'd planned to go there,' she explained, and he looked relieved that crowded town shops weren't to be their destination.

'They have a good restaurant,' Bryony coaxed, for Lance's devotion to his appetite was the opposite of his sister's.

They set off in her car, driving quickly through the winter lanes with their leafless hedges and muddy potholes.

'This is such a beautiful countryside in spring and summer,' said Lance, 'but it loses all its charms in winter.' He changed the subject abruptly. 'How are you enjoying the job? How d'you get on with Justin?'

'The job's fascinating, and so varied. I can't thank you enough for getting it for me. And, of course, it's permanent now.'

'Yes, I'd heard the dragon won't be coming back. And how do you get on with Justin?' he pressed.

Bryony considered. 'He's very kind,' she said at last. 'He gives me lots of interesting things to do, not just typing and filing. We go out sometimes to do research and . . . ' She stopped and coloured slightly.

'And you've fallen madly in love with him,' Lance teased.

'Oh, really, Lance!'

'Don't tell me you're not a bit smitten with him, famous author and all that,' he persisted. 'And he's very attractive to women, I believe.'

To her relief, Bryony saw the sign for the garden centre just ahead. She joined the queue of cars waiting to get into the car park and this manoeuvre enabled her to avoid any more conversation on the embarrassing topic of her feelings for Justin. She had no intention of confiding in Lance.

They walked quickly across the windy car park and entered the warm display area with relief. A cacophony of carols from speakers and toys assaulted their ears.

Lance gave a mock shudder. 'Come on, first stop coffee; it'll be quieter in the restaurant.'

It wasn't, but Bryony didn't mind.

'It's called Christmas atmosphere,' she said, looking at the huge tree with its twinkling lights and the strings of festive garlands and lanterns. 'I love it. It reminds me of my childhood when my dad and I used to visit the big shops on Christmas Eve.'

Then she remembered that Lance and Heidi had lost their own parents as children, and stopped.

'Heidi and I used to go with Nanny Flake,' he said cheerfully. 'Justin wouldn't come, of course.'

'He must have been very young when he became your guardian,' she commented.

'He was, but he shared the job with Aunt Norah in London. We stayed with her a lot until she became ill. And don't forget we both went to boarding school, so he only had to bother with us in the holidays. And, of course, there was always Nanny Flake and Mrs Buckley.' He grinned at her. 'We did very well, really.'

'Thoroughly spoiled, I expect.' With

his cheeky grin, Lance would have been the sort of boy women would want to spoil.

'I want to see the Pets' Corner,' he announced, wiping the crumbs of mince pies from his lips. 'I love rabbits, especially those little ones with long floppy ears.'

Bryony glanced at her watch. 'Give me an hour. You go and see the rabbits and I'll scour the place for something for Justin. Any ideas?'

'None at all,' said Lance cheerfully. 'He's got everything. I shouldn't bother. Just give him a big kiss.' He dodged away before Bryony could slap him.

Chuckling to herself, Bryony made her way to the gift section. What *would* Justin say if she gave him a big kiss for a Christmas present?

She wandered fruitlessly from section to section until, almost in despair, she found herself in the picture department. Amongst the wide range of prints, and even some original paintings, she spotted a display of black and white silhouettes, and in the centre, in an oval silver frame, was a lady in a sweeping gown and a large elegant hat. Underneath were the words *The Merry Widow*.

Bryony gazed at it, mesmerised. Bella! Could she find anything better for Justin? As if it might suddenly disappear, she plucked it quickly from the wall and took it over to the till. An efficient assistant replaced it and found her a new one in a box.

She was still smiling with pleasure as she made her way through the crowds to where she had arranged to meet Lance, the precious picture safely in her bag.

'You look pleased with yourself,' he observed.

'I am. I've finally found something for Justin.'

He glanced curiously at her bag but said nothing. Obviously she wanted to keep it a secret.

'Did you see the rabbits?' she asked.

'I did. They're gorgeous. In fact, I couldn't resist them so . . . ' He reached into his pocket and carefully drew out the head of a little fur rabbit. 'It's for you.'

'Lance! I don't want a rabbit! What on earth will I do with it?'

'Oh, but he's so cute — and desperate for a loving home. There, say hello . . . ' He drew out the whole rabbit and placed it in her cupped hands.

'Oh, Lance, you are an idiot!' She nuzzled the realistic little toy, stroking its pale imitation fur. 'It's lovely. Thank you very much. Shall we go back now? It's nearly lunchtime.'

'Mm. I have some visiting to do this afternoon. Don't want to lose touch with my local friends.'

He held the door for her and they went reluctantly into the cold car park.

They drove back, singing carols as they bowled along the country lanes, and were laughing as they blew into the hall at Greston Tower.

An astonishing sight met their eyes. Buckley, looking wobbly at the top of the stepladder, was attaching a golden angel to the top of a huge Christmas tree, while Justin held an armful of decorations and shouted instructions from below. Heidi and Simon were fastening red velvet ribbon bows to the staircase.

'What the . . . ?' Lance's face was a study. 'We *never* decorate like this,' he muttered to Bryony. 'Justin doesn't like it. Calls it 'tat'.'

'He said we'd have an old-fashioned Christmas,' she whispered back.

'Here, you two.' Justin had spotted them. 'Lend a hand. There're some holly branches over there. See what you can do with them.'

By dinner time, the house was aglow with lights and sparkle. Heavy mirrors reflected flickering candles and the dark wooden wall panels set off hoops and swags of fir cones and green and golden leaves. Justin, looking happy and relaxed, had supervised everything.

'He's like a different person,' Heidi whispered to Bryony in wonderment. 'D'you know what I think? I think it's because you're staying for Christmas.'

'Me? I don't think I'd make that much difference. No, he's cheerful because he fancied a traditional Christmas this year and for that you need a house full of people.'

★ ★ ★

On Christmas Eve, they all piled into Justin's car and drove to the church in the village. Golden light spilled out of the wide doors as they walked up the path, while the interior was bright with glossy winter leaves amongst which nestled red and white candles. There was an old crib and kneeling figures near the altar and a soaring Christmas tree below the steps.

The church was filling up as Justin led them to the family pew. He let the others pass into their seats then placed Bryony next to himself.

As they sang the beautiful familiar carols, Bryony was very conscious of Justin's nearness as they shared a hymnbook. The book was unnecessary; they knew all the words by heart.

Her companion last Christmas Eve had been her father. At the memory, tears filled her eyes, but Justin, smiling down at her, sensed the reason for her sadness and placed a hand over hers and gently pressed her fingers. At that moment, Bryony knew she didn't want to be anywhere else but with Justin in the little village church.

What if Heidi was right? Was he happy because she was staying for Christmas? Could he ever be interested in her, return her love?

Then Carla Willard's face came between them. Wait till I get back, she seemed to be saying.

As they came out of church, Bryony spotted Rowan in the crowd. He beckoned to her and, with a glance at Justin striding ahead with Lance and Simon, she whispered to Heidi,

'Wait for me, please.'

Rowan pressed a little box into her hand.

'Happy Christmas, Bryony. I'll be thinking of you.'

From her bag, she took a long, narrow parcel, brightly wrapped; crystallised ginger, his favourite, she knew.

'Happy Christmas, Rowan.'

She darted back to Heidi who looked at her curiously but asked no questions as she tucked the little box into her pocket to open later. They hurried and reached the car before the others could wonder where they were.

'Drop us off here, Justin,' said Lance at the gates of Greston Tower. 'We'll walk up the drive. It's a lovely night.'

They all climbed out leaving Justin to take the car to the house, and with linked arms began the walk under a bright, full Christmas moon. It was cold but they were well wrapped up.

'A Christmas moonlit walk.' Heidi squeezed Bryony's arm. 'How romantic.' She gave Simon a radiant smile from under her fluffy hat and he bent and kissed the tip of her nose.

Bryony thought again what a change love had brought in Heidi.

They came out of the tunnel of trees to face a house ablaze with warmth. Justin had switched on the lights in all the rooms facing the front, and was waiting in the hall with a big bowl of steaming, spicy punch, while Mrs Buckley appeared with plates of hot sausage rolls and mince pies.

'A midnight feast! Yahoo!' shouted Lance. 'Come on everyone, dig in!'

'We should open our presents now,' Heidi suggested. 'We're all wide awake.'

'No.' Justin was firm. 'After breakfast on Christmas morning — that's present-opening time. And if we don't get to bed soon, no one will be up for breakfast.'

Laughing merrily, the party made their way upstairs.

In her room, Bryony sat on the edge of the bed and took Rowan's little box from her pocket. She held it for a few moments, almost afraid to open it. What if it was a ring? Unlikely. Rowan had said they would discuss things after Christmas. But what if he couldn't wait, was sure she would change her mind?

There was only one way to find out. Carefully she removed the lid — and sighed with relief. It wasn't a ring but a small enamelled cat on a silver chain. The fur was ruffled and the eyes were two tiny elongated emeralds. It was exquisite.

She sat looking at it for some time. Dear Rowan. This was truly a gift of love. If only she could return his love, how simple life would be.

★　★　★

They all appeared bright, excited and wide awake at breakfast-time, then, when the meal was over, they adjourned to the drawing-room where a pile of interesting-looking parcels in colourful wrapping paper were piled under another decorated tree.

Justin refused to be Father Christmas, so Lance, in a red dressing-gown borrowed from Nanny Flake, which was way too short for him and barely met round his middle, did the honours.

Bryony watched anxiously as Justin opened his gift from her, but the delighted expression on his face told her that she had chosen well.

'She shall hang in my writing room to inspire me,' he told her.

Bryony opened his present to her. It was a porcelain lady — another Merry Widow. Tiny flowers peeped from the rich, red folds of the dress, the lace bodice looked real and golden jewellery decorated her fingers and neck. A broad-brimmed hat piled high with feathers and ribbons was tilted forward over her luxuriant hair.

Bryony gazed at the figurine, speechless. She had never owned anything so beautiful. She stammered her thanks, embarrassed that he would have given her such an expensive present.

'Why the Merry Widows?' asked Lance.

Justin shook his head and gave Bryony a secret smile. This was something between them alone.

There was a squeal from Heidi. 'Oh, what a wonderful present! I love it!'

She had removed the mirror from its box and was turning it this way and that, gazing happily at her reflection.

Later, once every gift had been opened and exclaimed over, the wrappings cleared away and a satisfying little stack of acquisitions piled by each chair, Lance jumped up and went to a cupboard. He returned with a large, flat box.

'It's still there,' he said to Heidi. 'Remember — every Christmas morning?'

'Of course — the jigsaw puzzle. Come on, everyone, we'll do it together. It's what we always did as children.'

They pulled up chairs to the big table where Lance tipped out the puzzle, and for the next hour there was teasing and laughter as the picture slowly took shape.

Justin, sitting near the fire with a new Christmas book, glanced up now and then, enjoying the scene.

No one heard the door open until Carla Willard was in the room. Bryony's heart sank.

'Happy Christmas, everyone.' She flashed a smile round the room, and her glance took in Bryony poring over some pieces of the jigsaw's sky. She took a step towards her.

'I'm surprised to see you here.' Carla's voice was icy. 'Didn't your family want you home for the holiday?'

'They've gone away. Justin invited me to stay here for Christmas.'

'Well, I suppose it's nice for Lance to have someone, too.'

Justin had risen and tried to draw Carla nearer to the fire, but she resisted.

'Let's leave the young people to their amusements,' she said with a brittle laugh. 'I want to tell you about my course. And give you your present, of course. Come on, we'll go to the sitting-room.'

As Bryony watched her take his arm and urge him towards the door, Heidi caught her eye.

'Don't worry, she won't be here for lunch,' she muttered. 'Justin told me she has people staying. She won't be here long.'

Bryony continued to work on the puzzle but her mind was in the sitting room. Was Justin in thrall to the other woman again, seemingly under her spell? And what could she do about it?

Finally, she heard Carla's car race away, but Justin didn't rejoin them, and for an awful moment she wondered if he had gone with Carla. But then the door opened and he entered with a little figure dressed in scarlet on his arm. Nanny Flake.

The young people fussed round her and she was soon settled by the fire, the mohair stole wrapped round her shoulders. She gave Bryony a special smile.

'I'm glad you're here,' she said quietly. 'Justin's very happy and I think you may be the reason. That Miss Willard is no good for him. Very selfish, she is.'

'Nanny comes down every Christmas to have lunch with us,' Justin explained.

At that moment, the gong sounded and they all went into the dining-room.

Lunch was to be their main Christmas meal because they had been invited to a party that evening, and Mrs Buckley had excelled herself. The table decorations were beautiful and the meal itself perfection.

Replete with turkey, Christmas pudding, and all the trimmings, they were talking quietly over nuts and glasses of wine when Lance stood up.

'Come on, Justin. Concert time.' He turned to Bryony. 'Justin always plays to us after lunch while we digest our wonderful meal. It's the only time of the year we can persuade him.'

Bryony looked at Justin, startled, remembering his reaction when he had caught her listening to him playing when she first arrived.

'Perhaps Bryony would prefer to do something else . . . ' he began, but she broke in, 'Oh, no, I'd love to hear you play.' She didn't say 'again'.

Justin played for half an hour and not a word was spoken as, grouped in comfortable chairs around the piano, they gave themselves up to the pleasure of the music. Nanny Flake beamed and patted Bryony's knee. Her pride in Justin was obvious.

In the early evening they went upstairs to get ready for the party.

'What are you wearing?' asked Heidi. 'The midnight blue dress?'

'I haven't quite decided,' Bryony hedged. She wasn't going to reveal her secret.

They parted and Bryony went straight to the wardrobe and brought out the beautiful dress Aunt Margaret had sent and which she had shown no one.

It was of emerald taffeta shot with

deep gold. The tight bodice had a halter neck and the skirt billowed out from a tight waist. It had the luxurious look of one of Anila's exotic saris.

She showered and made up her face with extra care, elongating her eyes till they resembled the little cat Rowan had given her. Then she slipped on the dress and startled herself with her reflection in the glass. She was striking, glamorous, so unlike her everyday appearance, and for a moment she felt she might be too conspicuous.

Then she took a few deep breaths to steady her nerves, told herself not to be so silly and added the simple gold necklace and earrings she had decided to wear.

She almost wanted Carla Willard to be at the party. The dress gave her such confidence she felt she could fight any number of Carlas for the man she loved.

At half past seven, she slowly descended the stairs. Everyone else was ready and waiting and four pairs of eyes looked up at her. Justin, handsome in his beautifully cut dinner jacket, came to the bottom of the stairs and took her hand.

'I'm speechless,' he said quietly. 'You look so beautiful.'

Her answering smile was dazzling. Life could hold no greater happiness than this.

Mistletoe And Wine . . .

Bryony was glad the party was to be held at Allerton Manor, the home of Colonel and Mrs Ralston. She had liked the elderly couple very much when they had dined at Greston Tower.

'Will Carla be there?' Heidi asked from the back of the car.

'No. She has a prior engagement.' There seemed to be no regret in Justin's voice.

They turned into the drive of the Manor where several more cars were disgorging groups of laughing, elegantly-dressed guests.

Justin led his little party into the house, and Bryony gasped. The entrance hall was breathtaking. The ceiling, rising to three floors above, was studded with tiny coloured windows. A wide staircase swept upwards and a gallery ran all around the first floor.

She was so over-awed by the place that she failed to notice the colonel and his wife receiving their guests and had to be drawn forward by Justin.

'So you're staying with Justin for Christmas,' smiled Mrs Ralston.

The colonel looked at her approvingly. 'He's a lucky man,' he said in his gruff voice and Bryony felt for a moment like a prospective bride.

'Come on, let's go upstairs,' whispered Heidi.

They left their wraps in a huge bedroom where a maid sat in the corner ready to help if needed.

'Your dress is stunning,' said Heidi admiringly. 'When did you buy it?'

'Aunt Margaret sent it.' Tenderly Bryony smoothed down the wide skirts. 'She did brilliantly to get an exact fit.'

'Justin won't even think of Carla when he looks at you,' Heidi declared, and, as the other girl flushed, she gave her a searching glance. 'You're in love with him, aren't you?'

As Bryony didn't answer, Heidi

persisted, 'Aren't you?'

Finally Bryony nodded. 'But if you breathe a word, I'll leave Greston Tower tomorrow and never come back!'

Heidi looked hurt. 'Of course I won't. Has Justin said anything?'

'Said anything?'

'Has he said he loves you?' the girl pressed.

'Of course not. He doesn't love me. Why should he love me? I'm just his secretary.'

Heidi looked sceptical. 'I don't think so, somehow.'

'You have a too vivid imagination.' Bryony fluffed up a few curls on top of her head. 'What about Carla?'

'He doesn't love Carla,' Heidi scoffed. 'She may love him, I suppose — though I doubt it. He's just a good catch and she doesn't want him to escape. Anyway, she's not here tonight. So see what you can do.'

Laughing, the two girls left the room, and Bryony felt the blood fizzing in her veins. Heidi was right. With Carla out of the way and the stunning new dress, she had a chance to impress Justin.

The three men were waiting for them at the bottom of the stairs — and clinging to Justin's arm was Carla Willard.

'I thought you had a previous engagement,' Heidi challenged her.

'Did you, darling? I changed my mind.' Carla smiled sweetly at them all, and the group moved off into the ballroom.

'Carla seems as determined as ever to get Justin,' Lance murmured to his sister.

'Well, we'll have to see that she doesn't succeed, won't we?' Heidi muttered through gritted teeth. 'Anyway, I think even he's getting tired of her. She *is* irritating.'

'Is he interested in anyone else?' he wondered, and without thinking, she glanced at Bryony.

Simon, sensing a sudden atmosphere, led Heidi on to the dance floor, while Lance gave Bryony a little bow and offered her his hand, and off they went, too, leaving Carla in possession of Justin.

Lance was a good dancer and they enjoyed three dances before returning to their table. Heidi and Simon were there, but there was no sign of Carla or Justin.

'I wonder where he's gone?' said Simon. 'And who's that woman who was clinging to him for dear life? Is she his girlfriend?'

Bryony explained Carla's position in Justin's life.

'That's why she breezes in and out of Greston Tower whenever she likes,' she added.

'He'd better be careful if he's not really keen,' laughed Simon. 'She's out to get him! Come on, young Bryony, can't let that gorgeous dress go to waste. Let's give it a twirl on the dance floor.'

Bryony looked back a moment later to see Justin standing alone at the table, and felt a sudden pang. If only he had returned a minute sooner, she might have been dancing with him and not Simon.

The dancing ended and there was a general exit towards the supper room. Justin came back alone to the table.

'I've been asked to join our hosts,' he told them. 'The colonel wants to discuss something. You would all prefer to be with the younger people, I'm sure, so I'll join you after supper.'

'Well, at least he's not with Carla,' Lance observed. 'She's over there with someone else.'

They looked across the room.

'Kurt!' exclaimed Heidi. 'She's with Kurt van Arne.'

At the buffet table a few minutes later, they found themselves next to Carla.

'Was that Kurt I saw you with?' Heidi's question was direct.

'Yes, darling, but don't be jealous. You have a very nice partner of your own.'

'I'm not jealous. I just wonder what

Justin will think.'

Carla shrugged. 'I'm not with Justin tonight. I decided to come to the party after all — it turned out Kurt's partner had let him down so we got together. Purely convenience.' She added a crab patty to her plate and moved away.

Bryony had heard the exchange and groaned inwardly. Not Kurt van Arne again! She'd hoped they had seen the last of him now that Heidi was happy with Simon. If Justin became annoyed it would spoil the evening.

At supper, Lance met up with a few old friends and introduced them to Bryony. One of them, a blonde young man called Rob, couldn't take his eyes off her and eventually asked if he could have the dance after supper.

It would have been impolite to refuse, so, supper over, Bryony found herself being propelled inexpertly round the floor by the flushed young man. He was very pleasant but when her toes had been mangled for the third time, she suggested they sat out and talked instead.

Looking relieved, he took her into the Edwardian conservatory which led off the ballroom where a Christmas tree in the centre glowed with tiny lights and jewelled baubles, and golden lights peeped from plants and foliage. The effect was magical.

'Shall we sit here?' Rob led her to a wrought-iron bench made comfortable with deep cushions.

He was amusing, with an inate charm, and Bryony found his company relaxing. But then, in the middle of a burst of laughter, she glanced across the conservatory to find Justin watching her.

With a feeling of guilt, she began to rise to her feet, but he turned on his heel and disappeared through the door.

She sank back in her seat, all merriment gone. Why should she feel guilty? She was doing nothing but sitting out with a pleasant young man, a friend of Justin's ward.

'I think I'd better go back.' She stood

up. 'The others will be wondering where I am.'

Rob was obviously disappointed but took her back to her table, where there was no sign of Justin — or Heidi.

'She vanished ten minutes ago,' Simon explained, plainly worried. 'Could you go and see if she's upstairs? She could be feeling ill.'

Bryony thought it unlikely but agreed to go and look, although the idea flashed through her mind that Heidi could be with Kurt. Please don't let it be that, she prayed.

However, as she skirted her way round the crowd of dancers on the dance floor, she bumped into Kurt.

'Bryony! I didn't know you were here. Will you have this dance with me?'

'I'm sorry, Kurt. I have to go upstairs to look for Heidi. She seems to have disappeared.'

'Well, we could dance as far as the door,' he insisted merrily, and with that he took her in his arms and they began to waltz towards the door.

She struggled in his arms. 'This is silly.'

'No, it isn't. It's a rehearsal to see how well we dance together.' They reached the door and he released her. 'I'll ask you again later.'

She left him and went into the hall — just in time to see Justin striding away on the far side of the room. Had he seen that silly charade in the ballroom? There was nothing she could do about it if he had. Was he following her around checking up on her? What was the matter with him?

She ran upstairs to the bedroom where they had left their coats, and found Heidi sitting in the armchair with her shoes off and her feet up on a stool.

'Heidi! Are you all right? Simon said you'd disappeared.'

She looked doubtful. 'Simon! Don't tell me he's worried.'

'Of course he's worried. So is Lance. Are you ill?'

'No, I'm not ill. I'm furious! Simon's my partner but Lance had to go and introduce him to Carol Wood — and you know what she's like!'

Bryony bit back her amusement.

'I'm afraid I don't. Who's Carol Wood?'

'A maneater if ever there was one!' Heidi's face was red and her lips were tightly held in a straight line.

'I'm sure Lance was only being friendly,' Bryony pointed out reasonably. 'Anyway, he and Simon are alone at the table now. There's no Carol Wood or any other girl.'

'She wanted to dance with him,' Heidi muttered. 'She tried to get him away.'

'Well, she didn't succeed. He's waiting for you and he's worried.'

'Good. Let him worry a bit longer. Go back and say you can't find me. I'll go down when he's *really* worried.'

Bryony looked at her, exasperated. What a silly argument! When it was supposed to be the season of peace and love. She left the room without speaking.

★ ★ ★

It was interesting looking over the balustrade into the hall beneath, and she strolled around until she came level with the top of a towering Christmas tree. She was studying the beautiful white and silver angel on the top when a voice spoke behind her.

'No partner?' She knew who it was without turning. 'You seem to have danced with everyone except me. Even Kurt van Arne.'

She remained standing with her back towards him.

'That's hardly fair,' she retorted. 'I haven't seen much of you all evening, either.'

Suddenly he gripped her arm and spun her to face him. He crushed her in his arms and his mouth pressed against hers in a fierce kiss. Her eyes blazed. This wasn't the love she had hoped for, this was a gesture of annoyance.

He set her back and, before she could speak, pointed upwards to a large mistletoe ball above their heads.

'A Christmas tradition, I believe,' he said through clenched teeth. 'It gives gentlemen a certain amount of licence.'

Bryony put her fingers to her bruised lips. 'Not licence to attack, though.'

'Hardly that.' He took her in his arms again and this time the kiss was tender. She responded completely.

He slid his hands up her arms and held her firmly by the shoulders. His face was close to hers, his voice a whisper: 'I can't go through it all again.'

Was he talking to her or to himself?

Before she could speak, he had released her, walked quickly away and vanished down the stairs.

Bryony retreated to the bathroom, where she examined her face in the mirror. Her cheeks were flushed and her eyes had an unnatural sparkle. Would anyone guess what had happened?

She splashed cold water on her wrists, patted powder on to the redness to subdue it and renewed the lipstick on her lips. Then she sat on the edge of the bath and waited until she felt calm enough to go downstairs. When she did, she would have to face Justin again. What did his actions mean? What did 'I can't go through it all again' mean? Did he love her? Did he believe she loved Rowan as Eleanor had done?

Justin, darling, if you only knew. The words, whispered inside her head, sounded as loud as if she had shouted them.

Heidi joined her as she finally went downstairs.

'I think I've waited long enough,' she said with satisfaction, then looked at her more intently. 'What have you been doing? Your face is flushed.'

'Is it? It's rather warm,' Bryony invented airily.

They made their way to the table where the three men were watching the dancers, but as soon as they saw the girls, Justin and Lance both jumped up and offered a hand to Bryony. With an apologetic smile at Lance, she moved into Justin's arms. Without speaking, they circled the floor, his arm tight around her waist, his lips resting on her hair.

For the rest of the evening, they all behaved normally. Colonel Ralston appeared and insisted on a dance with Bryony, then Heidi. Mrs Ralston made straight for Lance.

'People will think I have a toy boy,' she chuckled to Heidi.

'Did I imagine the scene upstairs?' Bryony asked herself. Perhaps Justin had been in the grip of some sort of madness. He wasn't drunk, she was sure of that. But she'd seen evidence of his uncertain temper on the night she arrived. He was an artist, she reminded herself, and artists often behaved strangely when their passions were aroused.

She was glad that Carla didn't make an appearance at their table. The other girl had gathered a group of young men around her at the far end of the ballroom and seemed happy to dance and flirt with them and ignore Justin.

'She's always trying to make Justin jealous,' Heidi pointed out. 'But it won't work. He's losing interest in her.'

Bryony glanced at Justin. Certainly he was deep in conversation with Mrs Ralston and seemed oblivious to what was going on.

At midnight, a loud banging on the front door startled everyone into silence. As the music ceased, Colonel Ralston addressed them.

'Ladies and gentlemen,' he said, 'would you please all return to your seats? I believe we have visitors.'

Bryony looked at Justin who was smiling broadly. 'Do you know about this?' she asked.

He nodded but said nothing.

The buzz of excitement around the room was silenced as a tall figure in a red coat and white beard strode into the room. He bowed to each side and raising his arms, declared:

'In come I, old Father Christmas
Welcome or welcome not.

I hope old Father Christmas
Will never be forgot.'

He bowed again to a round of applause, then a procession of figures with blackened faces followed him into the hall and stood in a ring.

'What's going on?' asked Lance.

'I know,' said Simon excitedly. 'I've read about this. They're mummers.'

'Mummers?' Heidi looked at him, puzzled.

'Yes, it's a mummers' play.'

Justin shushed them as the players introduced themselves in turn.

'I am Saint George, the noble knight.
I come from foreign lands to fight.
To fight the Turkish knight who is so bold
And cut him down with his blood cold.'

The tall player dressed as St George brandished his wooden sword fiercely to cheers from the audience.

The Turkish knight's rhyme was received with a chorus of boos. Then a very large man in a long dress, golden plaits and a pointed headdress caused hysterical amusement as he fluttered his eyelashes and flirted with the men in the audience.

'That's the Lady,' whispered Justin.

The Fool in cap and bells and the Doctor with his black bag introduced themselves, and then the fun began.

The knights fought, leaping around the room, shouting and clashing their swords until the Turkish knight lay dead. St George tried to clasp the Lady in his arms, but the Lady, who was bigger than him, lifted him off the ground and spun him round and round. The audience had tears of laughter in their eyes.

Then the Doctor, with incantations and mystic signs, announced that the Turkish knight was restored to life, and the audience, entering into the spirit of the play, cheered and clapped.

Finally the Fool, capering and walking on his hands, led the whole group as it circled the room to wild applause and filed out, Father Christmas last, bowing to left and right.

'That was wonderful!' Bryony exclaimed. 'I've never seen anything like it before.'

'Normally they would make a collection now,' Justin explained, 'but it wouldn't be right at a party so Colonel Ralston will make a donation.'

'Who are they?' asked Lance. 'What made the Colonel think of this as an entertainment?'

'The Turkish knight is his gardener. He and his friends revived the mummers' play to raise funds for charity. He suggested it to the Colonel as an unusual entertainment.'

'Well, it certainly was that.' Lance sat back in his chair, smiling broadly. 'I'd like to be a part of it. It looks fun.'

Colonel Ralston joined them and was congratulated.

'Great, wasn't it,' he said. 'I love to see these old customs preserved.'

'Is it medieval?' asked Simon.

'Some people think so. Some say it only goes back to the seventeenth century. No-one really knows. A house like this would have been visited by mummers every Christmas a hundred years ago.'

'Well, we all thoroughly enjoyed it,' Justin told him warmly.

'We'll dance for another hour then there'll be coffee and mince pies before people leave,' said the Colonel. 'I think coffee will sober everyone up — if they need it,' he added with smile.

Justin led Bryony to the dance floor once more.

'Have I told you how beautiful you look tonight? That is without doubt the most striking dress in the room,' he murmured in her hair.

Bless you, Aunt Margaret, said Bryony silently. She looked at Justin from under her eyelashes.

'I don't think you've mentioned it lately,' she teased.

'How remiss of me. Have you enjoyed yourself this evening?'

She looked up into his eyes. What about the scene upstairs? Had he forgotten it? Or were they to pretend it never happened? If that was what he wanted, so be it.

'I've had a wonderful evening,' she answered solemnly.

★　★　★

The next morning, everyone slept late, and Bryony arrived at the breakfast room to find only Justin seated at the table.

She had spent the night dreaming of an empty ballroom where she and Justin had circled endlessly round and round. Looking at him, she felt herself half in, half out of the dream.

'We seem to be the only ones who can cope with late nights,' he said with a smile, pouring her a cup of coffee.

She helped herself to bacon and scrambled eggs from the dishes on the sideboard, surprised to find that she was quite hungry.

Justin had finished his meal, and he waited until she had finished, too, before taking a deep breath and looking directly at her.

'Bryony, I must apologise . . . This is so embarrassing. I don't know what came over me. I must apologise for last night.'

'Please.' A deep flush came into her cheeks. 'Can't we forget it happened? I hate apologies and explanations.'

'But I fear I may have spoiled your Christmas.'

She sat looking down at the table-cloth, unable to speak.

'Bryony?' His voice was gentle.

'This is the first Christmas without my father,' she said quietly. 'I wasn't looking forward to it. But it has been so much fun. I've been so happy. Please don't talk about spoiling it.' She looked up and gave a little laugh. 'And it's not over yet. It's only Boxing Day.'

He reached across the table and she put her hand in his.

'Bryony . . .'

The door opened and they drew apart as Carla Willard breezed in.

'Justin! I thought you might still be in bed.' She glared at Bryony. 'Not disturbing anything, am I?'

She helped herself to coffee and stood in front of the fire with her cup and saucer.

'Won't you come and sit down? I can ring for fresh toast,' Justin offered.

'No, thank you. I rarely eat breakfast. Did you enjoy last night?'

'Very much,' said Justin. Bryony felt herself ignored by the other girl so didn't bother to answer.

'You seemed to be having a good time,' Justin went on.

'Oh, I was, you may be sure.' Carla smiled as if thinking of something she had no intention of sharing.

'Mr van Arne took you home?' Justin asked.

'He did. I arrived with him and I left with him. Purely convenience, of course.' She gave Bryony a frosty smile.

'You seem to have become very friendly with him.' Justin had risen and joined her near the fire.

'Not very friendly. Old friends are always the best,' she simpered, patting his cheek with her fingertips. 'So I've come to see you this morning.'

'I'm always pleased to see you, of course, Carla.' His voice was cool. 'But I understood you had people staying.'

'Only my brother and his wife. They do their own thing, I don't stay in for them. Did you enjoy the party, Miss Redland?'

'Very much, thank you.'

'I thought your dress was very — striking. Did Justin choose it for you?' Bryony blinked. 'Justin? No. Why?'

'Oh, it seemed rather sophisticated for you. Not what I would have expected you to wear. You seem to have simpler taste. It's a difficult colour to wear.'

Was she being complimentary or insulting? Bryony couldn't tell and wasn't sure how to answer.

Justin came to her rescue. 'Bryony looked beautiful. It was a lovely dress.'

Carla gave a slight sniff and changed the subject.

'Justin, a group of us are going to the Chateau tonight. They've refurbished the dining-room and I'm dying to see it. I've come to invite you to join us.'

She seated herself in one of the armchairs near the fire, crossed her legs and swung one elegantly-booted foot up and down. Her smile showed that she was confident of his acceptance.

Bryony glanced at Justin. If he went out with Carla, Boxing Night would be spoiled.

'I'm sorry, Carla,' he said, 'but I've already made other plans. I'm going out to dinner with my guests this evening.'

There was silence in the room. Then Carla stood up, drawing on her gloves, and gave Justin a tight smile.

'I see. Well, perhaps another time. Enjoy the rest of the holiday. Goodbye.' She swept out, leaving the door open.

Slowly Bryony got to her feet, crossed to the door and closed it.

'Well, that spoiled my surprise,' said

Justin when she returned to the table, 'but never mind. We're all going to The Mill tonight. Guy has finished the renovations and they opened in time for Christmas.'

Bryony experienced a tiny feeling of disappointment. He'd said 'all.' She'd hoped it might be just the two of them.

Lance and Simon, and then Heidi, arrived, yawning, for breakfast. When they were settled, Justin told them his arrangements.

'Not me, I'm afraid,' said Lance. 'I've made other plans for tonight.'

'Bring her with you,' said Justin smoothly.

'I can't, the party's at her . . . Oh, very clever!' Lance grinned.

'So it'll be just the four of us. Dinner and dancing on a minute dance floor.' He stood up. 'Well, it may be a holiday for some people, but I think I'll do some work.'

Bryony stood up too, but he motioned her to sit. 'I might need you tomorrow so enjoy today.'

'So, what are we going to do?' Lance looked at the others. 'Any ideas?'

'Simon and I . . . ' Heidi began. 'Well, Simon's going home tomorrow so . . . '

'So you'd like to spend time together today,' Bryony finished for her. 'We understand.'

Lance nodded. 'Off you go, my children. Enjoy yourselves.' He turned to Bryony. 'That leaves just us. What shall we do?'

'For a start, we could finish that jigsaw,' she suggested.

'Good idea. I hate to put a jigsaw away unfinished. Come on.'

In the drawing-room, they settled one on each side of the table. There was only a boring patch of sky to do but they worked away for half an hour in such a companionable silence that the ring of the telephone made Bryony jump.

'I'll get it.' Lance got to his feet. 'It's probably for Justin.'

But it wasn't. It was for him. Bryony

heard, 'No, I don't think so,' and then, 'Well, I'll try,' before he replaced the receiver and came back to the table.

'I used to belong to the clay-pigeon shooting club,' he said. 'A group of my old mates are down there now and want me to join them. How would you like to come along? It's fun.'

'I'd rather not,' said Bryony slowly. 'Thanks for asking me, but I'm not really the sporty type. I might spoil it for you. But you must go.'

Lance shook his head. 'I can't leave you here on your own.'

'I insist. And I shan't be on my own — I'm going up to see Nanny Flake. I haven't had a coffee and a gossip with her for a while and she does enjoy it. I mean it, Lance. Please go.'

'Well — if you're sure.' He was obviously anxious to join his friends.

When he had gone, Bryony sat looking into the fire. She felt like the last of the five little Indians. Everyone had vanished. It was as though she was alone in the house.

She stood up. She had told Lance she was going to visit Nanny Flake so that's what she would do.

* * *

'Bryony, it's you.' Nanny greeted her with obvious pleasure and pulled her into the cosy little room. 'I was just about to put the kettle on. Come and sit down.'

Bryony picked up Pickle, no longer a tiny kitten, and put him on her lap but he jumped down immediately and began to claw his scratching post.

'He's showing off,' said Nanny. 'Mr Justin bought him that for Christmas and he loves it.'

So Justin had bothered to find a present for Nanny's cat? I wouldn't have expected that, thought Bryony.

'Look at my present.' Nanny seated herself proudly in a comfortable-looking armchair, pressed a small lever at the side, and her legs were lifted up to a reclining position. Another touch of the lever, and her legs were lowered. 'It's so comfortable for watching television. I love it.'

Bryony was made to try out the new chair and praised it lavishly as Nanny glowed like her red jacket.

'You've worked wonders with Justin,' Nanny said when they were seated with their coffee.

'Me? What do you mean?'

Nanny looked at her shrewdly. 'I think you know what I mean.'

Bryony stirred her coffee in silence.

'He's in love with you,' said Nanny.

'Oh no,' Bryony protested. 'I'm sure you're wrong.'

'And you're in love with him. But neither of you wants to admit it.'

'Has he — has he said anything to you?' Bryony dared to ask.

'He doesn't need to,' Nanny told her. 'I know him well enough to see it for myself. He's been unhappy for a long time, but since you came, there's been a change in him. He told me yesterday that this is the best

Christmas he's had for years.'

Bryony looked at the old lady. 'All right, I admit it. I am in love with him. But I don't want him to know. Please don't say anything. It would put him in an awkward position. I can't believe he can love me. He's handsome and famous — why would he choose me?'

Nanny Flake smiled affectionately. 'You're modest to a fault, my dear. Have more confidence in yourself. You're pretty and kind and you love him. What more could he want?'

Bryony frowned. 'Would you call him possessive?'

Nanny considered. 'Generally, no. But perhaps where someone he loves is concerned . . . He always said he would never fall in love again, never put himself in the position where he could be hurt.'

'After Eleanor, you mean?'

'After Eleanor,' Nanny agreed. 'If he allowed himself to fall for someone again, I think he could be possessive.'

'At the dance last night he seemed to

be always watching me,' Bryony confided. 'And he commented on how many partners I'd had.'

Nanny smiled gently. 'Don't judge him too harshly. Being in love is a strange sensation for him.'

'You love him very much, don't you, Nanny?'

'I've looked after him since he was a baby, now he looks after me.' Nanny's face was softly tender. 'Yes, I love him very much. He's a wonderful, talented man. If you love him, he's very fortunate; if he loves you, you're the luckiest girl in the world.'

She saw the glint of tears in Bryony's eyes and bustled away to make some more coffee.

'I did think at first that Rowan would be the one for you,' she called over her shoulder.

'Rowan?' Bryony had almost forgotten Rowan for the past two days. 'Rowan is a wonderful friend, but nothing more.'

'He loves you too, though. It's almost

like the old triangle.'

'Please don't say that.' Bryony felt real distress. 'That was so tragic. Can't we change the subject? What other presents did you have for Christmas?'

She stayed for an hour while they discussed presents and the party the night before. When she left, the old lady gave her a hug.

'You're a good girl, Bryony. I'm so glad you came to Greston Tower.'

From Nanny's apartment Bryony went to her own room and put on a thick jacket and a hat. Although she felt bundled up in the warmth of the bedroom, outside it would be very cold.

She intended to walk and walk and think of nothing but the exercise of putting one foot in front of the other. She had come to Greston Tower to enjoy an interesting new job, yet in just a few months she had found herself at the centre of a love triangle.

'It's Not What You Think . . .'

Guy had changed the outside appearance of the mill very little. There was still a cobbled forecourt, and he had added ornamental iron railings and hanging baskets to windows at the front, but the red brick façade remained as severe as it had been for over a hundred years.

Inside, things were very different now it was The Old Mill Restaurant. Thick carpets and chandeliers gave it a luxurious ambiance. A wrought-iron circular staircase descended to the centre of the room. The walls and window drapes were an elegant blue-grey and the napery sparkling white.

Guy came to meet them, smiling broadly.

'How wonderful to see you all. Your

table is this way. I hope you like it.'

The table, in a shallow recess, stood against a tall window which reached to the floor. Outside, concealed lights illuminated a tumbling stream.

'The old millrace,' Guy explained. 'We had to demolish the wheel — it was dangerous — but we made a feature of the water.'

Simon looked around. 'If the old miller could come back, he'd have a shock,' he laughed.

'It's beautiful,' Bryony told him as she accepted a menu.

'You've worked wonders.' Justin smiled his congratulations. 'I remember coming here years ago when it was just a ruin. It doesn't seem possible it's the same place.'

Bryony studied the menu, pleased it was in English and not too long.

'I can never make up my mind,' said Heidi, 'and whatever I choose, I want whatever someone else has when it comes to the table.'

Simon smiled at her indulgently.

'Choose two things,' he said, 'then you can have whichever you prefer and I'll have the other.'

Justin looked at them in mock horror.

'Must you spoil her? We have to live with her when you've gone back.'

'Oh, don't talk about that,' begged Heidi. 'I want to forget he's going tomorrow. I'll be all alone.'

'Apart from Justin and Lance and me.' Bryony made a face at the other girl then turned to the menu again. 'We've had such a lot of lovely Christmas food I think I'd like something quite different,' she mused.

Eventually she chose smoked salmon and prawn parcels, followed by a lamb and rosemary roast. Once she had given the waiter her order, she looked around. The room was filling slowly but there was no one on the dance floor which was, as Justin had said, minute.

Following the direction of her gaze he stood up. 'Come on, Bryony, let's try the floor while we're waiting for our food.'

The music was soft and seductive and they drifted and swirled in perfect harmony, Bryony in an ecstasy of happiness as his arms closed firmly round her.

'The patrons probably think we're the cabaret,' Justin teased. 'Would you like to try some spectacular sequence to entertain them?'

She looked at him in alarm. 'I don't know any spectacular sequences — do you?'

'Actually no. But I can see two waiters approaching our table, so we can make our escape.'

The food was delicious, the service good but unhurried, and at the end they all sat back, happy and relaxed.

'When we can move, we'll dance again,' Justin suggested.

'What a wonderful end to Christmas,' said Simon. 'I have enjoyed myself. Thank you so much for inviting me, Justin.'

A waiter approached with a tray of coffee, followed by Guy with a serious look on his face.

'There's a call for you from the Tower,' he said to Justin. 'Would you like to take it in my office?'

As Justin left the table, the others looked at each other in concern.

'Not Lance,' said Heidi in an agonised tone. 'Or Nanny!'

Simon reached for her hand. 'Don't imagine things. Wait till Justin gets back to tell us what's happened.'

When Justin returned after a few minutes, Heidi looked at him beseechingly. 'Please tell me nothing's happened to Lance?'

'No, it's Aunt Norah. She's had a stroke. It's not the first, but they don't think she'll get over this one. I'm sorry to break up the party but we'll have to go to London first thing in the morning so perhaps we should go back now and pack a few things.'

Lance had also been summoned and was waiting for them when they got home.

'Poor Aunt Norah,' he said. 'What time shall we leave in the morning?'

'I'll leave at the same time,' said Simon, 'then I'll be able to say goodbye to everyone.'

He and Heidi went upstairs with their arms round each other, Lance following behind.

Justin looked at Bryony.

'Don't worry about me,' she said hastily. 'I'll be fine with Mrs Buckley and Nanny Flake.'

He took her hands. 'I'm sorry to leave you here, but I don't think you'd enjoy a hospital vigil, especially when you don't even know Aunt Norah.' He looked into her eyes. 'Bryony, when I come back, we must talk.'

She opened her mouth to speak, but he shook his head.

'Not now. When I come back.' With another searching look, he turned away. 'Don't get up for us in the morning. We'll be off very early. I'll phone from London.'

★ ★ ★

The next day was the loneliest she had
spent since arriving at Greston Tower.
After breakfast, she wandered from
room to room, wondering how to fill
her time and missing the others more
than she could have imagined.

Justin had left a pile of notes and a
few letters for her attention, but she
finished them in no time and wondered
what else to do. She took out the box of
photographs, but put them away almost
immediately. Her mind was in London
with Justin; she couldn't concentrate on
anything else.

When the telephone rang mid-
morning, she raced to answer it. It was
Simon.

'I've just got home. Any news from
London?'

'Nothing yet. Are Aunt Margaret and
Uncle Chris back from Austria?'

'No. The house is empty. Good thing,
too. I've got two reports to finish. They
should be back tomorrow, though. It

was a good Christmas, wasn't it?' His voice was warm.

'Wonderful. I'm glad you came.'

'You seem very happy there,' he observed.

'I am. I feel as if I belong.'

'I'm glad. I'll see you again in a few weeks. I promised Heidi to come up again as soon as possible. Look after yourself.'

She replaced the phone and sat looking into space. The room was quiet again. Justin's words replayed themselves inside her head: 'When I come back, we must talk.'

She was sure he hadn't meant talk about the book, or about Heidi and Simon. If Nanny Flake was right, he would talk about their future; ask her an important question.

She knew what her answer would be. She closed her eyes and tried to remember the feel of his arms about her as they had danced at The Old Mill Restaurant. Darling Justin, she whispered, come back soon. I miss you so much.

Justin rang after she had finished a lonely dinner on a tray in front of the television in the cosy sitting-room. It was Mrs Buckley's idea and Bryony was grateful to accept. She hated the empty public rooms with their abandoned Christmas trees and forlorn decorations. The television took her mind off her lonely state.

'Aunt Norah has rallied a little,' said Justin, 'but we can't come home just yet. Are you all right on your own?'

'I'm fine.' She forced her voice to sound bright. 'But I will be glad when you're all back.'

He talked for a few minutes longer, then wished her a conventional goodnight. She guessed others were within listening distance.

Feeling faintly dissatisfied, she made her way upstairs. She would have an early night, perhaps a long bath and then bed with a book. She was re-reading all Justin's novels.

However, before she reached the top step, Mrs Buckley called up to her.

'Miss Redland, Miss Willard was on the telephone asking for Mr Darke. I told her he's in London for a few days.'

'Thank you, Mrs Buckley.'

Bryony continued along the corridor. Well, at least I won't be bothered by Carla Willard, she thought. If Justin's away, she'll find someone else to irritate, I hope.

* * *

The next morning, on her way to breakfast, Bryony heard voices coming from the little passageway which led to Justin's music room. Curious, she crept towards the door and silently pushed it open.

Standing behind a tripod, Kurt van Arne was adjusting a camera directed at Justin's piano. Carla sat in an armchair in her favourite position, knees crossed, one foot swinging up and down, laughing so loudly that she failed to hear the door open, so that Bryony was standing in front of her before she realised someone had entered the room.

'What are you doing?' Bryony's voice registered her total incredulity.

'Oh, it's the secretary.' Carla dismissed her with a wave. 'I thought you'd gone to London with Justin. How can he possibly manage without you?'

'I said, what are you doing?'

'What does it look like?' Carla drawled. 'Haven't you seen a camera before?'

Kurt ignored them and changed his position.

'But Justin will be furious!' Bryony declared. 'He's absolutely against this, you know he is. He told you so.'

Again Carla waved that dismissive hand. 'This is a surprise for Justin. I don't think he realised what he meant. He'll be thrilled once he sees the prints. Kurt is a marvellous photographer.'

'He will not be thrilled and you know it!' Bryony returned icily. 'I think you should stop now and go.'

She found she wasn't overawed by

either of them. Her concern was wholly for Justin and what he would think when he returned. He might even ask why she hadn't stopped them.

Carla stood up. 'I don't think we want your opinion, thank you. You're a newcomer here and — may I remind you — only a secretary. We'll go when we're ready. I shall soon be mistress here anyway, and you'll be the one who will go then.' She turned her back on Bryony, stalked to the armchair farthest away, and sat down again.

Bryony looked at them both in despair. What could she do? She couldn't phone Justin; he had worries enough in London.

Leaving the room with as much dignity as she could manage, she went into the breakfast-room. But she couldn't face more than a piece of toast and a cup of coffee. If only there was something she could do.

She decided to get some fresh air and, well wrapped up, strolled across the drive and into the shrubbery. The morning was crisp and dry with faint shafts of wintry sunshine through the branches.

Becoming aware of twigs cracking behind her she looked round and found Rowan following her.

'Bryony! I saw you from Nanny's window. She said everyone had gone to London. Why are you here alone?'

'They've gone because Lance and Heidi's aunt has had a stroke. But there was little point in my going since I don't know her. They may be back tomorrow.'

He linked his arm through hers. 'Poor thing. No wonder you look so glum. Would you like me to take you out somewhere and cheer you up?'

'No, thanks, Rowan. It's very kind of you but I want to stay here in case there's a call from London.'

They strolled on towards the lane. Rowan withdrew his arm and put it round her shoulders, drawing her close. 'Bryony, I have something to tell you. I'll be leaving here in three months.'

'Leaving? Where are you going?'

'To Africa, with an international aid team. I'll be away for about two years.'

She stared at him incomprehendingly. 'But . . . you asked me to marry you.'

'If we married, we could make it a honeymoon,' he returned thoughtfully. 'But we won't be getting married, will we?'

'What do you mean?' She looked startled. 'Has Nanny been saying anything to you?'

'Nanny doesn't need to tell me what I can see with my own eyes,' he said softly, and she looked away from him. 'Justin and I were rivals in love once before,' he went on quietly. 'I won't fight him again.'

They had reached the lane and were turning to go back to the house when a car raced down the drive and sped past them out of the gate.

'That was Carla, wasn't it?' Rowan exclaimed. 'Who was with her?'

She longed to confide in him and ask his advice but instinctively felt it would be the wrong thing to do.

'I didn't see anyone,' she said. 'Come on, let's go back and get a hot drink to warm us up.'

He gave her a curious glance but asked no more questions.

When they reached the front door he said, 'I won't stay for coffee if you don't mind. I have things to do.'

'You're not — angry, are you, Rowan?'

'My dear girl.' He bent forward and gave her a light kiss on the forehead. 'You know the old saying, all's fair in love and war? That's the way it goes. Justin's won this time. See you soon.' With a wave, he was gone.

★   ★   ★

Bryony spent the rest of the day worrying about the scene in the music room. She considered phoning Carla, but as quickly dismissed the idea. The other girl would enjoy knowing that Bryony was upset and unable to do anything.

After dinner, she made a decision. She would tackle Kurt instead. She knew where he lived. She would go to his house and plead with him to give her the prints or destroy them.

However she knew she had made a mistake the moment he opened the front door of his cottage. His cheeks were red and he gripped the edge of the door to steady himself. Obviously he had been drinking — heavily.

'Miss Redland! Bryony! This is a surprise. Come in, come in.' He pulled her inside. In a panic she tugged back towards the door but he held her arm firmly and swept her along a passage and into a sitting-room, strikingly furnished and decorated in black and white.

'I was all alone and wishing for a companion and look what the fairies left on my doorstep,' he burbled.

'I'm not staying . . . ' she began.

'Not staying! Of course you're staying. We'll have a little party, just the two of us. What would you like to drink?' He weaved his way to a well-stocked sideboard and stood looking expectantly at her.

'Perhaps coffee would be a good idea,' she suggested. 'I'll make it, shall I?' She moved towards the door in search of the kitchen. If there was a back door there she would abandon her mission and escape.

'No! No coffee! You can't have coffee at a party. Wine, that's the thing. Sit down, Bryony. I'll give you a glass of wine.'

She perched on the edge of an armchair and watched him warily. This had been a huge mistake, but she must keep her head. Talk to him. Pretend to be friendly. Perhaps she could still persuade him.

'Kurt,' she began. 'Those photographs you were taking this morning at the Tower . . .'

'Come and sit by me.' He patted the sofa.

Reluctantly she joined him and tried again.

'Justin really will be furious when he finds out. Carla's wrong about them. If we destroyed them . . .'

Kurt burst out laughing. 'Destroy them! You must be mad! I have great plans for those prints.' He moved closer and put an arm round her waist, and she turned away from his fume-laden breath. 'You know, you've got a very good figure. I could take some lovely photos of you — if you know what I mean,' he leered at her. 'And we wouldn't tell Justin — or Carla. Our secret.'

Bryony felt sick. She just had to get away. No one knew she was here so no one could help her. She had to help herself.

She forced a smile. 'What would I have to do?'

'Good girl. We'll enjoy ourselves. Drink up your wine and I'll get the studio ready. I won't be long.'

As soon as he left the room, Bryony darted to the door and peeped out into the corridor. Good, there was no sign of him. She crept along the passage to the front door. There was a click as she opened it but she hoped he was too far away to hear.

Then she was racing down the path, through the gate and up the lane to her car. She flung herself inside, switched on the engine and raced away.

The twisting lane came out on to the road which led past Greston Tower, and as she sped along, a car came up behind her.

When she turned into the drive, the following car did the same, and instinctively she knew who was behind her. Justin had returned.

She pulled up outside the garages and jumped out, relief and happiness on her face.

'Justin, you're back! I'm so glad!'

'And where have you been?' His face in the security light on the garage wall was stern.

'I just — I went for a drive,' she fibbed.

'I saw you turn out of High Top Lane. There is only one house in that lane. It belongs to Kurt van Arne. And it's a dead end.'

What could she say? Could she tell him what had happened? Would he believe her? She knew Carla and Kurt would deny her story if they were challenged. And if Kurt decided to destroy the prints after all, or Carla had a change of heart, there would be no need for Justin to know anything.

He took her hesitation for guilt.

'Bryony, I'm so disappointed in you. I came back early because I hated being away from you. I thought you would be waiting for me, but instead . . . '

'But, Justin . . . '

'I've heard the girls flock around him but somehow I thought you were different.'

She was close to tears. 'I can't explain now, but it's not what you think.'

He looked at her reproachfully. 'Perhaps you can bring yourself to explain in the morning. Goodnight, Bryony.'

That night, desperately unhappy, she cried herself to sleep.

'I Need Your Advice . . . '

Bryony arrived in the breakfast-room next morning just as Justin was leaving, so she was spared the ordeal of sitting opposite him in silence or trying to make conversation.

'I may head back to London in an hour or so,' he said, once he had given her a cool 'Good morning'. 'I've left a list of questions on your desk. If it's convenient, would you go down to the County Record Office and see if you can get some answers?

'Also, Mr Pryor-Brown, my solicitor, has a box of family papers I told him we'd collect them after Christmas. Perhaps you could call in for those, too?'

He had gone before she could answer.

She ate her breakfast thoughtfully. These were the sort of errands she enjoyed, but if she and Justin were to continue working together, his coolness would make it very difficult.

Christmas was over. The glamour, the dressing-up, the fun were all behind them. Now it was back to work. But so much had happened over the holiday, so many different emotions had been aroused, it would be difficult to get back on to their old footing. Had she been wrong to stay for Christmas?

She stirred her coffee absently, wondering what to do. He hadn't mentioned last night. Should she tell him exactly what had happened and risk the consequences? Should she carry on as if nothing had happened and hope he would come round eventually? Or should she leave?

Leave Greston Towers? Leave the interesting job and all the friends she had made? Above all, leave Justin?

She would never stop loving him, but could he really love her when he seemed unwilling to trust her? Without any real grounds for suspicion and certainly no proof, he had decided she had deceived him with Kurt van Arne.

She pushed the coffee away and stood up. If she decided to leave, she owed it to herself to tell him the truth first. For now, she would carry on as if nothing had happened.

She went into the library and collected the papers he had mentioned from her desk. She looked up Mr Pryor-Brown in the address book and noted where she would find his office. Then she set out.

The morning was wet and cold, and reflected her mood. She climbed into her car and set off through the dripping countryside to Worcester.

The Record Office was in a back street. She had been there before with Justin. She parked the car and threaded her way through busy shoppers pouring in and out of shop doorways. Christmas panic had been replaced by sales frenzy in just one week.

She turned off the shopping area, made her way through an arcade and some twisty back streets and reached the Record Office.

Inside, she entered her name and address and the purpose of her visit in the register, then she studied Justin's list and began to select maps and directories to answer his queries. She felt proud that she only needed to ask for the archivist's help with one question.

She worked diligently for an hour, then, satisfied, put her notebook and several sheets of photocopied paper into her briefcase. She was pleased with her work and hoped Justin would be too, until she remembered that he was annoyed with her. But she wouldn't think of that. She'd find somewhere for a quiet cup of coffee before looking for Mr Pryor-Brown's office.

It had stopped raining and after ten minutes' walking, she found a café opposite the solicitor's office.

The café was small but clean and cheerful, and as she looked around for a seat, she heard someone call her name.

'Coo-ee, Bryony.' It was Fiona, the wife of Andy, Rowan's friend. 'What a bit of luck. I was hoping I would bump into someone. Are you shopping? If you are, we could go together. There are some really good sales on. I've already got lots.' She patted a carrier bag at her side.

'Actually I'm working,' Bryony explained once she'd ordered coffee, 'not shopping. I can only stay for a quick coffee.'

'Oh, shame. Rowan came to supper last night,' she announced. 'He told us his news. Has he told you, or shouldn't I have mentioned it?'

'About Africa? Yes, he told me.'

Fiona gave her a coy look. 'You're not going too?'

'Me?'

'Well, we thought — that is, you and Rowan seemed very friendly. We'd like to see him get married again.'

Bryony shook her head. 'Rowan and I are good friends, that's all,' she said firmly, and something in her tone silenced Fiona who picked up her coffee cup and began to discuss shopping.

Bryony drank her own coffee quickly and was soon outside again. Fancy bumping into Fiona! Well, if she had been hoping to glean some gossip, she had been disappointed, she thought as she crossed to Mr Pryor-Brown's office.

The box was ready for her to collect. Mr Pryor-Brown wasn't very busy and would have enjoyed a chat with Justin's attractive new secretary, but Bryony, inexplicably disgruntled after her encounter with Fiona, merely gave him a pleasant smile and left.

Back at Greston Tower, all was quiet. Justin must have returned to London. And perhaps it was as well. A few days' reflection away from her might bring him back in a better fame of mind.

In her room, she removed her hat and tidied her hair. As she did so, she had an idea. Perhaps Nanny Flake would like to come down and have lunch with her for a change.

She went up to Nanny's room and was surprised to find the door slightly open. Nanny never wandered around the house, so perhaps someone was with her. Probably Mrs Buckley with the lunch tray, she decided.

She pushed open the door and called gently, not to startle the old lady if she was on her own. There was no reply. She was venturing towards the sitting-room when a familiar voice pulled her up short.

' . . . too much to hope that she could be as loyal and sweet as she seemed at first.' It was Justin.

'You've got the wrong idea somehow, lad. You always were impetuous, even as a child.' Nanny sounded cross. 'She's a lovely girl and I know she loves you.'

Cheeks flaming, Bryony held her breath. If Justin discovered her here, he really would think she was untrust-worthy. Listening in to other people's conversations would rate very low in his opinion. She crept back to the door.

'After all this time, I really thought

I'd found someone . . . ' Bryony fled along the corridor before she could hear any more.

There were voices in the hall below. Coming up the stairs were Heidi and Lance.

'What's up?' asked Lance when he spotted her. 'You look as if you've had a shock.'

Bryony glanced back over her shoulder towards Nanny Flake's door. There was no sign of Justin.

'It's nothing — really.' She rallied quickly to smile at them. 'You two are back early. I thought you were staying in London and that Justin was rejoining you today.'

'We changed our minds,' Lance explained. 'We rang him just after breakfast. Aunt Norah's doing really well — against all odds — so we decided to come back. But Justin will go up again next week.'

'Have you heard from Simon?' Heidi's face was eager.

'Yes. He's at home, working hard.'

'Well, he'll have to stop for ten minutes and speak to me because I'm going to phone him right now.' She pushed past them and made for her room.

Lance grinned. 'I think your cousin's made quite an impression,' he said. 'Heidi chattered about him all the way home.'

'Lance, can I talk to you?' she asked suddenly, and he blinked in surprise.

'Of course. Talk away.'

'Not here. Can we go out somewhere?'

He glanced out the window. 'It's raining again so walking's out of the question. But we could go to the Red Lion in the village, or the café.'

'No, not the café. I want somewhere where we won't be overheard. I need your advice.'

He looked intrigued. 'Of course. But I must just report in to Justin first. Do you know where he is?'

'He's with Nanny Flake.'

'Right. I won't be long.'

'Lance.' She grasped his arm. 'Don't mention me. Don't say we're going out.'

He looked at her curiously. 'Something's wrong, isn't it?'

'I'll wait for you in my car,' she said, not answering.

★ ★ ★

The Red Lion was arranged in little alcoves and corners, perfect for private conversation. Lance ordered coffees and small brandies to warm them up and once they were settled near a huge log fire, he looked at Bryony expectantly.

'Christmas was wonderful,' she began, 'not least because Justin and I seemed to be coming to a special understanding.'

'You mean, he fell in love with you?'

She looked down at her hands, nervously twisting her fingers together.

'So what's the problem?' he pressed. 'Don't you love him?'

'Oh yes.' The words were out before

she could stop them. 'But something happened yesterday and he's become cold and distant again. He — he thinks I'm interested in Kurt van Arne, of all people.'

Lance looked incredulous. 'Why on earth should he think that?'

Bryony sighed. 'I'd better tell you the whole story. Then you can tell me what you think I should do.'

Lance listened without interrupting as she went over all of the events of the day before; finding Carla and Kurt taking photographs in the music room, worrying all day, and finally visiting Kurt at night — with its disastrous consequences.

'With his reputation, that was a risky thing to do,' he commented.

She grimaced. 'I realise that now, but at the time it seemed like the best solution. I thought we would talk and he would understand and destroy the prints.'

Lance shook his head. 'You *are* an innocent.'

'Thanks, Grandad.' Her eyes flashed. 'So, tell me what you think I should have done.'

Lance took a sip of his brandy as he considered.

'Talked to Carla?' he suggested.

She shook her head. 'Not a chance. She hates me. She thinks I'm trying to take Justin away from her. Of course, he never belonged to her, but she can't see that.'

She picked up her coffee cup and put it back, untasted.

'I barely knew Kurt, but when we met he seemed polite and friendly,' she explained. 'If I thought anything at all about him, I thought I could at least trust him. But I suppose when I turned up on his doorstep he imagined I could be a new conquest.'

'What an unlucky coincidence that Justin appeared just when you were turning out of High Top Lane,' Lance observed and she agreed with a wry grimace.

'The only car on that road and it had

to be his! He was bound to put the wrong interpretation on things.'

'But he knows you and he loves you. Why didn't he give you a chance to explain?'

Bryony shrugged. 'I couldn't explain without telling him everything. So I just looked guilty.'

'But *they* were in the wrong, not you,' he pointed out.

She made no answer.

'You haven't touched your coffee. It must be cold.' He stood up. 'I'll get two fresh ones.'

Bryony gazed into the deep-burning logs with their flashes and sparks. As a lonely child, she had been cheered and comforted by the castles and animals she could imagine in the fire's redness. What a pity it couldn't provide a solution to her problem now.

'Do you think I should leave?' she asked as soon as Lance returned with fresh coffee, and he looked up, startled.

'Leave? Leave Greston Tower? Certainly not! If you do, they've won.'

'Then what should I do?'

'Would you like me to speak to Justin?' he offered, but she shook her head.

'No. I think I must fight my own battles. I just want your advice.'

'Then I think you should stay and carry on as if nothing's happened,' he said decisively. 'Things have a habit of working out. I'll bet those two beauties will come unstuck somehow. And Justin's not stupid — he'll soon see Carla for the scheming madam she is. You can't possibly leave. Justin needs you.'

Bryony gave a weak smile. 'Thank you. I think I'd already made that decision myself. I just wanted you to confirm it.'

'So I've been wasting my time,' he said in mock annoyance. 'Come on, drink up. We might as well get back.'

★ ★ ★

Raised voices from the library were audible as soon as they entered the house. They looked at each other uncertainly.

'Looks like they're coming unstuck earlier than I expected,' he murmured with some satisfaction.

'What shall we do?' she whispered back.

He winked mischievously. 'I think we'll join them, don't you?'

'Oh, no, Lance!' She held his arm. 'I couldn't go in.'

'You can and you will,' he said, putting an arm firmly round her waist, and he ushered her towards the library door.

Inside, Carla was lounging in an armchair trying to look unconcerned. Justin and Kurt van Arne faced each other across the table. Between them were spread out twenty or more large photographic prints.

The three of them glanced up as Lance and Bryony came in, then continued their argument while they watched in silence. Bryony was glad of the support of Lance's arm.

'You're telling me that against my express wishes, you came here and photographed my private rooms?' Justin's voice was quieter now but he was incandescent with rage.

'But, Justin, darling . . . ' Carla began, but he spun round and glared at her.

'You *knew* how I felt about this, yet you broke in . . . '

'Oh, hardly! Mrs Buckley let us in.'

'There was no invitation. I was away. Therefore I say you *broke* in and wandered around my house taking photographs.' He turned away, struggling to control his fury.

'But if you would just look at them,' Kurt pleaded. 'Published with a well-written article . . . Think of the publicity. That sort of thing boosts sales every time.'

Justin turned back to him. 'Without wishing to sound conceited, my sales are more than satisfactory, thank you. I don't need that sort of cheap publicity.'

With a sudden movement, he snatched

up several of the prints, tore them in half and threw them on the fire.

As Kurt put out a hand to stop him, Justin snatched up the rest of the prints and burned them, too.

There was silence in the room now, except for a few crackles from the grate.

'I'll give you until tomorrow evening to hand over all copies and the negatives,' Justin finally said quietly. 'I shall make my solicitor aware of this incident and take advice. If necessary, I shall sue. Now — get out of my house.'

Kurt looked at Carla, who shrugged.

'Off you go, Kurt,' she said languidly. 'I'll see you soon. Justin and I have to have a little talk . . . '

Justin turned to her. 'No, we don't. We have nothing more to say to each other — ever. I want you to go — now.'

For a second she looked at him as if she couldn't believe her ears, then she picked up her bag from beside her chair and slowly got to her feet. Without hurrying, she crossed the room and stood in front of him.

'Very well. I wish you luck with your milk-and-water secretary and her desire to do good deeds.'

Without another word, she walked towards the door, paused to look back scornfully at Bryony, then swept out.

Justin waited until he heard the front door close behind them, then turned wearily to Bryony.

'What did she mean by 'desire to do good deeds?'

'You've been very unfair to Bryony,' Lance put in hotly. 'Let her explain.'

Justin looked irritably at Lance's arm which still held Bryony tightly.

'You don't have to protect her. I'm not dangerous. Bryony, will you please explain?'

Bryony threw Lance a look of appeal. 'It'll be easier if we're on our own while I try to explain. Would you mind — ? But thank you.'

Once she was alone with Justin, Bryony walked over to the fire and faced him.

'I'll tell you what happened yesterday

and why you found me coming from Kurt's house. But if you don't believe me, it will be best if I leave.'

Once again, she recounted the events of the day before, her eyes never leaving his.

At the end, he gave a deep sigh. 'My darling girl, can you ever forgive me?'

At the expression on her face, he opened his arms and she went into his embrace, her eyes glinting with tears.

'You won't leave,' he whispered, 'not now, not ever. I can't imagine my life without you. I love you so much.' He looked into her eyes. 'Could you really love me?'

'I think I've loved you since the moment we met.'

'And I've been so horrible to you. I thought you were in love with Rowan. I fought against my feelings for you. I couldn't bear to lose another girl to him. You've made me so happy.' He covered her face with kisses.

'Rowan has been a wonderful friend to me, but it's you I love. It always was,' she whispered.

'Darling Bryony, will you marry me?'

Their lips met and he had his answer.

★   ★   ★

The next day, Bryony and Justin went upstairs to see Nanny Flake. 'It's only fair to tell her before we make it public,' said Justin. 'Though I'm sure she'll have guessed the story would end like this.'

Nanny opened the door, took one look at their faces and flung her arms round them both.

'I knew it! You've come to your senses. I'm so happy. Come and tell me what made you change your minds.'

Once again, Bryony went through the story of Carla and Kurt's illicit photography session and her dangerous visit to Kurt at night.

'You see — I knew there would be an innocent explanation for that,' Nanny commented to Justin. 'She's a brave girl and she did it for you.' She patted Bryony's knee. 'I needn't ask if you're happy. I just have to look at your faces. Now I can die content. My Justin settled with the girl he loves.'

'What's this about dying?' laughed Justin. 'You've got to come to our wedding first. And you must choose a beautiful new outfit. My present to you.'

'Red, of course,' smiled Bryony. 'I'll take you to town and help you find something.'

Nanny smiled a self-satisfied smile and twinkled at Justin.

'Now I have a surprise for you. I was to give it to you on the day you told me you would be married. Wait here.'

She bustled into her bedroom next door and they heard drawers being opened and closed. Soon she was back holding a small parcel.

'Almost forgot where I'd put it!' she said as she handed it to Justin.

Bryony watched as he removed the brown paper. Inside was a small carved wooden box. He raised the lid to reveal something wrapped in brightly patterned silk.

They looked at each other. 'Anila,' breathed Bryony.

Justin handed her the silk bundle. 'You unwrap it,' he murmured.

Slowly she removed the soft material. Inside lay the flower pendant set with tiny emeralds worn by the Indian girl in the painting. She touched it tenderly with one finger-tip. 'I can't believe it.'

'There's something else.' Justin lifted an envelope from the bottom of the box and extracted two slightly faded photographs, one of a beautiful girl in a sari, her thick hair flowing almost to her waist, the other of a middle-aged couple with the same girl sitting between them. On the back was written *'Andrew, Bella and Anila.'*

Bryony studied the three people who had fascinated her ever since she had arrived at Greston Tower. Now, as a little family group, they came to life.

She could picture them living here as she did now.

She hoped her future would hold more happiness than Anila's had done. Unlike Anila, who had not found love, she had found it with Justin. Her future happiness would be safe.

Bryony and Justin looked at each other, then at Nanny.

'Who . . . ?' he began.

'It was Rowan, wasn't it?' Bryony's thoughts had jumped ahead of his.

Nanny nodded. 'It has been in his family since it was given to his father on his wedding day. When his parents died, it came to Rowan. Now he thinks you should have it.'

'But I never knew . . . ' Justin began. 'And why should he give it to us?'

Nanny looked directly at Bryony. 'You know that Rowan is going to Africa, which can be a very dangerous place. It's possible he might never come back. But also, he thinks he'll never marry again.'

As Bryony looked down at her hands,

Nanny added, 'He doesn't blame you, you know that. But he thought that you and Justin should have the box and pass it on to your children.'

Justin took Bryony's hand and held it tightly.

'So our marriage has solved a family mystery — the whereabouts of Anila's jewels.'

'It wouldn't have been a family mystery if you and Rowan had mended your differences,' Nanny put in, her voice gentle but reproachful.

Justin gazed into the fire without speaking. Then he got to his feet and held out a hand to Bryony. 'Come on, we have a lot to do if this wedding's ever to take place.'

He bent and kissed Nanny. 'Thank you for being the messenger and, please — thank Rowan for his gift.'

As they went back down the stairs, Bryony wondered whether it would be the right time to broach the subject of a reconciliation between the cousins. But she decided to wait for a while. Nanny had sown the seed; it might germinate in Justin's mind without her help.

Later, she added Rowan's name to the list of wedding guests.

However, Rowan returned thanks and an apology. He would be at a meeting for his new position on that day and unable to come.

Perhaps it's all for the best, she thought.

★ ★ ★

On a Spring morning three months later, Bryony, a radiant bride in billowing white lace, left the church on Justin's arm. Against her throat glowed a delicate gold flower pendant set with tiny emeralds. She carried a bouquet of deep gold roses nestling in vivid green leaves. Justin, in morning dress, looked more handsome than ever.

Mrs Buckley wept into a handkerchief.

'I can't help it,' she sobbed to Nanny Flake. 'They make such a beautiful couple.'

Bryony had insisted on the wedding being held at the village church and the reception at the Tower.

'I want to be like Bella,' she said to Justin. 'Aunt Margaret and Uncle Chris understand.'

Aunt Margaret, elegant in soft blue with a blue and cream flower-laden hat, had beamed with pride from her place at the front of the church. She was enchanted with Justin, and when he gave her a personal tour of the gardens and promised her several plants to take home, she couldn't praise him enough.

Despite Justin's desperate attempt to keep the wedding quiet, news had leaked out, and there was a group of agitated Press photographers at the gate.

'Very well, just a few, then please leave us alone,' he bargained.

The photographers clicked frantically then drifted reluctantly away.

Behind the group, Bryony spotted someone watching.

'Justin.' She held him back as he lead her towards the wedding car. 'There's just one thing I'd like you to do to make the day perfect.'

'Anything. Name it.'

'You might not be pleased,' she warned.

He looked at her serious face then turned to look at the man walking towards them. After the slightest hesitation, he held out his hand to Rowan who grasped it eagerly. A moment later, the two men were hugging each other tightly.

Heidi, a picture in her bridesmaid's dress, flung her arms round Bryony.

'You've done it! You've ended that dreadful feud.'

Rowan looked at Justin. 'May I kiss your beautiful bride?'

'Of course. She was your friend before she was mine.'

Rowan put his arms around Bryony and kissed her forehead twice.

'Dearest Rowan,' she said. 'Come back to us safely.'

He took her hand and passed it to Justin.

'The best man won,' he said simply. 'I know you'll make each other happy.'

THE END

We do hope that you have enjoyed reading this large print book.

Did you know that all of our titles are available for purchase?

We publish a wide range of high quality large print books including:
Romances, Mysteries, Classics
General Fiction
Non Fiction and Westerns

Special interest titles available in large print are:
The Little Oxford Dictionary
Music Book, Song Book
Hymn Book, Service Book

Also available from us courtesy of Oxford University Press:
Young Readers' Dictionary
(large print edition)
Young Readers' Thesaurus
(large print edition)

For further information or a free brochure, please contact us at:
Ulverscroft Large Print Books Ltd.,
The Green, Bradgate Road, Anstey,
Leicester, LE7 7FU, England.
Tel: (00 44) **0116 236 4325**
Fax: (00 44) **0116 234 0205**

Other titles in the
Linford Romance Library:

DARK MOON

Catriona McCuaig

When her aunt dies, Jemima is offered a home with her stern uncle, but vows to make her own way in the world by working at a coaching inn. She falls for the handsome and fascinating Giles Morton, but he has a menacing secret that could endanger them both. When Jemima is forced to choose between her own safety and saving the man she loves, she doesn't hesitate for a moment — but will they both come out of it alive?

HOME IS WHERE THE HEART IS

Chrissie Loveday

Jayne and Dan Pearson have moved to their dream house . . . a huge dilapidated heap on top of a Cornish cliff. The stresses of city life are behind them, their children consider their new home 'the coolest house ever', and the family's future looks rosy. But when a serious accident forces them to re-think their dream, they embark upon a completely different way of life — though its pleasures and disasters bring a whole new meaning to the word *stress* . . .

A HATFUL OF DREAMS

Roberta Grieve

Sally Williams works in a milliner's salon, but her ambition is to own her own shop. When she delivers a hat to Lady Isabelle Lazenby, she becomes flustered by Lady Isabelle's handsome cousin, Charles Carey — but finds herself attracted to the footman, Harry. However, Charles' interest in Sally causes a rift in her friendship with Harry, who also seems to be close with Maggie, Lady Isabelle's maid. Will Sally achieve her ambition? And could there be a future for Sally and Harry?

LOVE GAME

Diney Delancey

Rowena Winston had enjoyed working with her dear friend Donald. Together they had turned Chalford Manor into an excellent hotel and country club. But now Donald was dead, and she had the far greater challenge of working with his younger brother Clive — a man who had every reason to resent her!